THE CHRISTMAS FOUNDLING

A CHRISTMAS REGENCY ROMANCE

MARTHA KEYES

PARADIGM PRESS

The Christmas Foundling © 2020 by Martha Keyes. All Rights Reserved.
All rights reserved. No part of this book may be reproduced in any form or by any electronic or mechanical means including information storage and retrieval systems, without permission in writing from the author. The only exception is by a reviewer, who may quote short excerpts in a review.
Cover design by Martha Keyes and Ashtyn Newbold.

This book is a work of fiction. Names, characters, places, and incidents are either products of the author's imagination or are used fictitiously. Any resemblance to actual persons, living or dead, events, or locales, is entirely coincidental.
Martha Keyes
http://www.marthakeyes.com

To Micah and Jonah:
You were worth the wait

To Zachariah:
I know the wait to meet you will be worth it too

AUTHOR'S NOTE

This book delves into a topic near and dear to my heart, as it is something I've personally experienced. Infertility is crushingly difficult in any age, but the Regency era, with its focus on heirs and successions, would have heightened the pain for both women and men in many ways.

Everyone experiences adversity differently, but I hope that those who have gone through infertility—or still are experiencing it—will feel themselves represented and heard in pieces of this story.

I hope that those who do not have personal experience with this topic can also benefit from and sympathize with the situations portrayed in the book, even if they are fictional ones.

Finally, I hope that the story conveys the hope of the Christmas Season, particularly in a year when, like Lydia and Miles's story, things will likely play out differently than we had hoped. There is joy and growth to be found even amidst such trials.

CHAPTER 1

There had rarely been a colder December in England, yet it was not the frigid cold out of doors which made the hands of Lydia Blakeburn tremble in her dressing room as she stared at the letter she held. Lydia didn't *want* to end her marriage, but this letter might well tell her if it was possible. And if it was possible, it seemed her duty to do so. For her husband's sake.

She clenched her eyes shut and broke the seal. There was little point in prolonging her anxieties.

My Lady Lynham,

I was honored to receive your communication dated the thirteenth of December. I am afraid that I have little to add to the general knowledge you already possess, but perhaps my words will clarify any misunderstandings that may yet exist. As you implied in your letter, grounds for divorce are generally limited to adultery on the part of the wife. It is a lengthy, costly, and public process to see through, of course, and many couples choose to settle for divortium a mensa et thoro, which allows husband and wife to live apart—both physically and financially—without the option of remarrying.

Annulment is available for a wider range of issues, and the inability to perform one's marital obligations is a consideration, certainly, but requires an investigatory process that most people find entirely too distasteful and humiliating to subject themselves to. If you—or your friend—wish for more information on that, I can provide it. However, lack of offspring in and of itself is not grounds for divorce. That is rather left in the hands of God, as is only proper.

Otherwise, an annulment can be granted in cases of a marriage improperly performed—banns not being read, errors on the marriage license itself, etc.—a minor marrying by license and without permission, bigamy, or one of the parties not being in their right mind at the time of the marriage.

I hope you—and your friend—find this information useful. I beg you will not hesitate to respond if you have any further questions.

Yours,

James Coates

Coates & Lamming, Solicitors

London

Lydia swallowed painfully, blinking to dispel threatening tears. Never would she have thought to be inquiring on such matters, and she hardly knew whether to be relieved or disappointed by the solicitor's response. She had harbored little hope that her inability to provide her husband with an heir would be enough to legally justify an end to their marriage, but there was an element of defeat in the news all the same. She didn't know how much longer she could continue as they were.

And yet, the prospect of an annulment made her sick to even consider. To make five years of marriage as though they had never happened at all? And it had all started with such promise, such hope, such joy. In those days, she and Miles had spoken of children like foregone conclusions, looking to the future in all its hazy but certain bliss.

A soft tap sounded on her door, and she hurried to fold up the letter, placing it in the drawer of the table before her.

"Come in," she said, stretching her mouth into a more pleasant expression.

The bonneted heads of her two sisters, Diana and Mary, appeared in the doorway.

"Are you ready yet?" Diana slipped into the room, and Mary followed behind, the smiles on their faces evidence of how they regarded the prospect before them.

Neither of them seemed terribly disappointed at being stuck in London, which was a relief to Lydia. They had both been looking forward to going to Lynham Place for the duration of Christmastide, but a journey all the way to Staffordshire was out of the question, given the state of the roads. Reports claimed they were sheets of uneven ice—when they weren't covered in snow. Fog, too, had hung over London for many days now, making travel even in Town treacherous. Thankfully, it had lifted yesterday. But the cold remained.

They were to go out in it all the same. Lydia was determined to make her sisters' time in London as enjoyable as possible, even if it meant enduring a bit of censure from her mother-in-law and an evening of frozen fingers and toes.

"Yes, I am ready." Lydia rose from her chair and pulled on her wool pelisse. "Or as ready as one can be to go out in *that*."

They all looked toward the window, its pane covered in a latticework of frost.

"We shall simply have to eat and drink our fill of wassail and mutton to keep warm," said Diana, handing Lydia her bonnet.

Mary rubbed her hands together in anticipatory delight and slung an arm through Lydia's, pulling her from the room.

The three of them were met on their way down the corridor by Lydia's husband, Miles, who had just come from his own bedchamber. He wore a great coat, and a black top hat covered his blond head of hair. He was as handsome now as he had been when Lydia had first set eyes on him, and yet, so much more unattainable in many ways, given the gulf that had widened between them.

As his gaze moved between the three sisters and settled on Lydia, she saw it in his eyes—the momentary hesitation as he debated how to treat his wife in front of her sisters. Lydia didn't want Diana or Mary to know the troubles they had come upon. She didn't want to burden their time here with any of that.

Miles sent Lydia a smile and offered her his arm. "I believe my mother awaits us."

Lydia looked at him. "I thought she was set against the expedition."

Miles gave something between a smile and a grimace. "You know her. She is simultaneously offended by and interested in such affairs. I imagine she has found consolation in persuading herself that she is acting as a sort of chaperon."

Lydia didn't doubt it. The dowager would never take her seriously as a capable adult until she was also a mother. Five years into marriage, that was looking highly improbable.

"The truth is," he said in a conspiratorial whisper directed at Lydia's sisters, "that she is too curious to pass by such an opportunity."

"I cannot say I blame her," Mary said. "I understand it has been nearly two decades since the last Frost Fair. Perhaps our having to stay in Town for the season will be a blessing in disguise."

Lydia mustered a smile, but she had great doubts on the subject. She had been looking forward to their time in Staffordshire almost as much as her sisters had. London was so full of people with endless questions, conjecture, and advice to offer. Always unsolicited.

A footman pulled open the door, and a gust of chill wind swept around them, bringing on a collective shiver. Diana and Mary seemed thrilled with it, though, and charged ahead, not even waiting for Miles to help them into the coach that awaited.

He handed Lydia up, though, not meeting her eyes. She stifled a sigh. Long gone were the days when every touch was full of significance.

The dowager baroness, a regal if somewhat plump woman in her early fifties, had lodgings only two streets away, a fact which had given Lydia ample room for regret over the course of their time in Town. She was a frequent visitor—and often an unexpected and unannounced one—in their Mayfair townhouse, and though she was polite to Lydia, Lydia had never been able to forget how little her mother-in-law had wished for the match between Miles and her. It had not been the brilliant match she had hoped he would make.

Ever thoughtful and attentive, Miles retrieved his mother from her doorstep and escorted her to the coach, where she settled in next to Mary and Diana.

"A more miserably cold day has surely never dawned," she said as she arranged herself in the seat. "I wondered if you might have thought better of your intention to go to the fair, but if you are set upon it, I cannot help but think it best that you have someone with you who has experience with such an event."

Lydia tried to suppress a smile, and immediately her gaze went to Miles, whose eyes held laughter. As their gazes met, though, his smile faltered slightly.

It happened frequently these days—this awkwardness in their interactions. Neither of them knew what to do with these moments of shared amusement and understanding. They felt like memories of a bygone past, slipping unsolicited into the present.

"We are obliged to you, Mother," he said.

She smiled kindly then straightened suddenly. "Oh, I had meant to tell you, my dear"—she looked at Lydia too—"of a new physician I heard about the other day. He is apparently very well-versed in"—she cleared her throat—"matters that concern you. He has some treatments that you might wish to look into."

Lydia's cheeks flamed, and she gripped her hands together in her lap, avoiding the eyes of her sisters and husband. The helpful suggestions of her mother-in-law were never easy for her to accept, but even less so in the presence of her sisters.

"What is his name?" Miles sounded mildly interested, and Lydia tried to force herself to relax, feeling her sisters' eyes on her. She sincerely wished Miles wouldn't encourage his mother in her interest in their affairs, though. So much about their situation was humiliating enough already.

"Doctor Russell," his mother replied. "I am certain I could arrange for him to see you—"

"Thank you, Mother. Lydia and I will discuss it and decide how to proceed."

She could have kissed him right then in gratitude, but that would hardly have been appropriate. Besides, it was not something they did anymore, kissing.

The streets surrounding Blackfriars Bridge were swarmed with carriages and people making their way to and from the river. Mary's and Diana's heads crowded the coach window in their eagerness to catch a glimpse of it all.

"How splendid!" Diana cried out.

"Good heavens!" Mary said. "Is that a real live elephant? I suppose we needn't worry about the ice breaking under us, at least."

There was nowhere to leave the coach standing in such a place, so the coachman let them down just shy of the bridge. The bitter air nipped at any exposed skin it could find, and Lydia adjusted her fur-lined coat to cover as much as it would while the group of them made their way through the thick crowds and down the slope, covered in snow. Someone had set down flagstones to pave the way, and Miles handed each of the four women down then paid the waterman with a handful of jingling coins for their entrance.

Secure on the bank of the river, Lydia looked at the ice with a flutter of nerves. The river buzzed with the chatter of everyone standing upon it. She was not particularly timid, but she had never walked on ice before. How much weight could it possibly hold?

Mary and Diana stepped onto the river and, with all the confidence in the world, turned and gestured to Lydia. "Come, Lydia," said Mary. "If an elephant can cross the Thames, none of us need fear!"

"Not until *after* Christmas dinner, at least," Diana said significantly.

Lydia laughed to cover her nerves and watched as her mother-in-law stepped onto the ice, helped by her son. Diana raised a brow at Lydia in a good-natured challenge.

"It is silly, I know," Lydia said. "But, be the ice ever-so-thick, one would imagine that, at some point, the weight upon it would simply be too much. Particularly given the number of fires one sees lit upon it." Across the expanse of the frozen Thames, a dozen stacks of smoke billowed into the nippy air.

She felt her hand suddenly taken up. With a hint of a smile, Miles held her gaze and nodded, encouraging her forward while keeping a firm hold on her hand. It was her favorite smile of his—the one he believed he was concealing. But she'd had five years to become acquainted with his every expression.

She allowed him to pull her gently forward, and with her feet squarely on the ice, he tucked her hand into his arm.

With each step, Lydia's confidence grew, and soon, her fears were forgotten with the appeal and novelty of the sights surrounding her: a group of children kicked a ball to one another, a stack of pamphlets sat on a table next to a printing press, a hock of ham hung above a fire as a man rotated it slowly.

A child sat on the ground, hand to his head, while a neatly dressed doctor attended to him.

"Must have slipped," Miles said, following her gaze. "I imagine Dr. Kent has his hands full caring for injuries here. Plenty of opportunity for them."

As they threaded their way through crowds, bumping shoulders with merchants, fine ladies, schoolboys, and even a farmer leading a heavy hog on a rope, a host of smells competed for their attention. Wine, mutton, and smoke permeated the air from bank to bank. All of London appeared to be in attendance, with red-tipped noses that emitted puffs of fog with each breath. It was an invigorating atmosphere, and the air felt less oppressively cold with the hum of energy around.

And yet, amidst it all, Lydia's eyes seemed trained, whether she willed it or not, to notice one thing above all others. There were more babies than she had anticipated seeing in such frigid weather, and she wondered whether Miles noticed them as readily as she did. Or if they affected him the same way. With every baby she glimpsed, wrapped tightly in blankets and cradled in its mother's arms, she felt that familiar sting of longing and pain—of an emptiness that couldn't be filled by a cup of wassail or a plate of roast mutton.

CHAPTER 2

DECEMBER 23, 1813

Miles bowed low over the hand of his wife, trying to maintain a serious expression. Couples made their way over to the ballroom floor behind him as instruments strummed in preparation for the dance. Lydia was in high spirits this evening, and, whether it was due to the anticipation of Christmastide or something else, he fully intended to capitalize on it. Happy days for Lydia were getting fewer and farther between.

"May I have the pleasure of this dance?" he asked, brushing his lips on the back of her hand and looking up at her to gauge her response.

Lydia's eyes twinkled merrily, and she shook her head.

Miles straightened and drew back, surprised. Lydia never refused a dance. "May I know why I am thus snubbed?"

Her smile stretched larger. "I am not feeling well."

Miles couldn't stifle a confused chuckle. "You appear to be feeling very well indeed."

She tilted her head from side to side. "Well, I am, and I am not."

Her eyes sparkled mischievously at him. "Would you care to know why?"

He narrowed his eyes at her. He loved the playful Lydia, but it had been a long time since she had made an appearance. "I think so."

She motioned for him to come closer, putting a hand to her mouth as though she wished to whisper her answer. Her other hand reached for his, making his heart stutter. She so rarely initiated such contact these days.

"I believe," she whispered in his ear, and he could hear her smile, "that it is your child who is making me feel too ill for dancing."

He stilled, and she drew back, looking at him with wrinkles of joy around her eyes. He searched her face for any sign that she might be teasing him. But she would never. They were so far past the subject being a matter that allowed for any humor at all.

"You...you are in earnest?" he asked.

She nodded quickly and glanced around them before saying in an undervoice which trembled with excitement, "It has been almost seven weeks since my courses. And I have been feeling terribly tired and a bit nauseated." Never had such words been said with so much bliss.

He grasped her hands and brought them to his mouth, shutting his eyes as he pressed his lips to them. A baby! After four long years, a baby.

"But, Miles," she said urgently, "I don't wish to tell anyone just yet."

"Of course," he said hurriedly, clasping her hands tightly against his chest. It was all he could do not to kiss her then and there, in full view of everyone in attendance. It would have to keep until they returned home.

"A very merry Christmas indeed, my love." he said. By next Christmas, he would have an heir.

❄

The Present

To an unobservant eye, the woman about to brush by Miles and his family would simply appear dressed well for the cold. But Miles was not unobservant. And nor was his wife. Even if he hadn't known that the bundle of wool in front of the woman held a baby, he might have gathered as much just from the way Lydia's gaze followed her.

His heart sank. There were reminders of their pain everywhere.

Part of him wished he knew what thoughts were in Lydia's head right now, but he also dreaded knowing. He hated that Lydia couldn't have the one thing she wanted more than anything in the world: a baby of her own. And every time they shared a happy moment together, invariably it seemed to be followed by a reminder of that fact.

He had always assumed he would be successful—a successful baron, a successful husband, a successful father. But here he sat at thirty years old, with no child to call him "father," an unhappy wife, and no prospect of an heir. A failure at all three.

"Lynham!"

He turned to the voice and smiled at the sight of his friend, Edmund Goulding. "Goulding," he said as they shook hands. "Glad to see you here!" He glanced around. "Where is your wife?"

Goulding's mouth broke into a grin. "Can you keep a secret?"

Miles nodded.

Goulding leaned in. "She's in the family way again. Commissioned me to come here for some of the roasted chestnuts she loves. She can't seem to stomach much else right now. I could take her an entire cartload, and it would be gone by Epiphany! She is convinced it is a girl this time."

Miles glanced at Lydia. She and the others were browsing the wares of the nearest merchant. Thankfully. The last thing she needed was to know that the Gouldings would be welcoming a second child into their home. They had married two years to the day after Miles and Lydia. It had been a tender moment when they had learned of the Gouldings' first pregnancy. Miles could still remember the way Lydia had tried so valiantly to show unalloyed joy at the news.

"Congratulations are in order, then," Miles said with a friendly pat on Goulding's back. "Please give her my best wishes—and Lydia's too, of course." He glanced at Lydia again, and her eyes were on him, slightly curious.

He smiled and looked away, not wanting for her to come over. She would discover the news soon enough, but Miles didn't want it to be tonight. "I think I saw a man selling chestnuts just over there." He pointed Goulding in the direction of the merchant.

"Thank you, Lynham." He raised his brows with a provocative smile. "And I hope to be congratulating *you* soon." With another wag of the brows, he left.

Miles's smile faded as quickly as did his view of Goulding. He sighed and turned toward his family, who were admiring the carved wooden figures of a passing peddler. Mary debated over which one to purchase and settled on a figure of St. Paul's Cathedral.

They continued on their way, strolling past the various tents and stalls that ran the length of Blackfriars Bridge. Men and women called out to them, offering a game of nine pin bowling, hot apples, and sweets. Diana pleaded with them to stop for some gingerbread, and no one had any complaints at the suggestion. The scent of fresh, warm gingerbread was more than Miles felt capable of refusing.

Treats in hand, they walked at a leisurely pace along the row. At the end, backed up nearly under the bridge itself was a small hut constructed of sticks, with straw strewn all over the ice. People stood under its shelter, dressed in robes and looking down at a manger. Beside it all, a man recited verses from the second chapter of Luke, his voice ringing out loud and unmistakably Irish.

"Good heavens," said Miles's mother with an uncomfortable glance. "Of all the things. Are we to be overrun by Catholics, then?"

"I quite like it," Diana admitted unabashedly. Lydia had warned him that her sister's expectations for Christmastide were high. She was not refined enough to look down upon the festivities or displays his mother and others deplored.

"Is that a real baby?" Mary asked, craning her neck to see better.

"No," Lydia said. "It is only a doll."

Trust her to differentiate immediately.

"Thank heaven for that," said his mother. "It is far too cold for *any* baby to be out and about, though I have seen a number of them despite that." She glanced at the display again and primmed her lips.

"*And this shall be a sign unto you*," cried the man, extending the pamphlet in his hands toward Mary. "*Ye shall find the babe wrapped in swaddling clothes, lying in a manger.*"

Mary accepted the pamphlet with slight hesitation, and Diana took it from her and opened it, letting her eyes run over the words. The man returned to his place and continued his recitation.

"It is only more Bible verse," said Mary. "And information about the time and location of Christmas mass. Not a terrible souvenir, I suppose. Would you put it in your reticule, Lydia? It shall be crushed in mine, I think."

Lydia took the pamphlet from Diana and slipped it into the reticule dangling from her wrist, not meeting the disapproving eye of Miles's mother.

Diana and Mary led the way forward, and Lydia seemed content to let it be so. In the company of her sisters, she was in better spirits than Miles had seen her in for months. It had been a difficult year. Christmastide had always been a joyful time—a season for family and home and a reminder of the time of the year when they had married. But the joy had gone sour last Christmas, and things simply hadn't been the same since.

Diana and Mary seemed to be helping Lydia forget that, though, and Miles envied them their ability to put such a smile on his wife's face.

They stopped for some time to warm their hands over a fire which blazed forth from a copper tub, and they only turned away when Diana spotted a nearby printing press.

"Let us see if this is a better memento than the nativity pamphlet," she said. "I wish to never forget tonight, but I was not overly fond of the poem being printed at the last press we saw. I could never abide Pope."

The printer looked to be in the process of gathering up his things, but he gladly handed Diana a sample of what he was offering. She looked over it with critical, narrowed eyes.

"You may have the final printed copy, if you wish," said the man. "A full ten pages, miss. Three poems, the history of frosts—all the way since the year 200 A.D.—and the story of a woman who lived in a house made of snow."

"Delightful!" Diana reached into her reticule and handed the man two coins.

He took them from her and bowed, returning to the work of cleaning up. Most of the merchants seemed content to stay as long as there were people to buy their things, but the temperature was dropping, and a few were clearly of the same mind as the printer and had begun loading their things into carts and baskets.

Soon, Miles and the others came upon a fiddler playing a merry tune and a half-dozen couples dancing around in the space before him.

Diana turned toward Mary and grabbed her hands. "Come! Be my partner," she said, though she didn't give Mary much of a choice. They skipped around together, trying to imitate the couples around them with questionable success that brought a smile to Miles's face.

"Join us, Lydia! Come, Miles!" Diana called out amidst laughs.

Miles looked to Lydia, who met his gaze with mixed uncertainty and anticipation in her eyes. She loved dancing as much as her sisters did.

His heart beat more quickly as he extended his hand. He had been rejected so many times in the past—always with kind excuses—but somehow he could never resist an opportunity to hold her close. "Would you do me the honor?"

She smiled back at him and nodded subtly, sending his heart thudding against his chest at the unexpected response.

"Do be careful," said Miles's mother, clenching her teeth.

"Of course." He led his wife toward the dancers, putting an arm about her small waist and hoping she couldn't feel its trembling. What man who had been married five years shook at the prospect of dancing with his own wife?

But Lydia looked every bit as nervous as he felt when she set her hand on his shoulder. It was rare that they touched in anything but the most brief and superficial ways these days. Not long after the disappointment of last Christmas, they had argued, and Lydia had slept elsewhere. It had remained that way since.

Slowly, she had not only passed up opportunities to share his bed but any displays of affection at all.

There was a yelp, and Miles whipped his head around in time to see Diana land on her back and Mary tumble after her. The fiddling stopped, and so did the dancing.

Carefully holding Lydia's arm, Miles hurried with her over to Diana and bent down. "Are you hurt?"

Diana tried to push herself up on her elbow and winced, setting a hand to her side. "I can't decide if it is my hip or my pride which hurts more."

"You padded *my* fall, at least," Mary said with a teasing smile as she used Lydia's help to stand.

"I am moved by my own kindness." Diana stayed propped on her elbow, touching the back of her head gently.

"Did you hit your head?" Miles asked.

"Only slightly. It is just a bit tender."

He frowned. "Perhaps we should find a doctor. Dr. Kent is a good fellow, and I saw him here earlier."

She waved off the suggestion and pushed herself up, putting out a hand in invitation for Miles to assist her. "No, no. I am perfectly well, just a bit bruised."

"At least sit down for a moment over here," he insisted, guiding her slowly toward a large log near the river bank.

"Yes, dear," said Miles's mother. "You must certainly take some time after such a fall as that." She nodded at the fiddler, and he glanced at Diana before turning away and beginning the music again.

Miles's mother insisted that Diana stay seated for quite some time, and only Mary's suggestion that she and the dowager baroness bring back some hot chocolate resigned Diana to the prospect. Lydia stayed with her and Miles, seated beside Diana on the log, and Miles was selfish enough to regret the timing of Diana's fall for what it had deprived him of. It had been a long time since he had held his wife so close, and he didn't know when the next opportunity would arise. If at all.

They seemed to have settled into a routine that felt, to him, similar to what it would have been to marry for convenience rather than love. They didn't argue, at least. Indeed, sometimes he felt crushed by the civility they showed one another. He would have gladly taken a fiery debate with Lydia if it meant the prospect of reconciliation afterward, but since their last argument, she hadn't shown any desire to repeat the experience.

His mother and Mary's quest for hot chocolate took much longer than anticipated, and the crowds were beginning to thin by the time they returned.

"We are very sorry," Mary said, scurrying toward them as quickly as the ice and the mugs in her hands would allow. "We had a difficult time finding it, and, as it turns out, the tent where this was being sold was clear back near where we first entered. We were obliged to give the man a few shillings as surety that we would return these cups." Both she and Miles's mother held two mugs, and she gave one to Diana. The dowager baroness handed one of hers to Miles and took a sip from the other one in her hand.

Miles opened his mouth then shut it. "Here." He gave his mug to Lydia, who shook her head.

"*You* have it." She smiled and gently pushed it back toward him.

"Will you share with me?" he asked.

She raised her brows, and he chuckled. They had shared drinks before, and it most often ended with him apologizing. He took much larger swallows than Lydia. "I promise to be very controlled." He demonstrated with the barest of swallows then handed it to her.

From the vantage point the log afforded them, they all drank their hot chocolate, watching the scene before them and the people who had seen fit to attend the Frost Fair, in all their varieties.

"Perhaps we should be heading back," Miles suggested. "I imagine it will take some time for Gerrard to bring the coach around."

They made their way back toward the Blackfriars end of the fair, empty mugs in hand. It was cold enough now that Lydia's hold on his arm was tighter than before, and Miles blessed the frigid air for it. Perhaps he needed to see that fewer fires were lit at the house.

They came upon the nativity scene, but the people were all gone now, and only the hut of sticks, the straw, and the manger remained.

Lydia stiffened beside him, and the dowager baroness stopped.

"Do you hear that?" his mother asked.

"Hear what, Mother?" he asked with a hint of impatience. There was still a great deal of noise permeating the icy air, with merchants gathering their things. Soon, only the tents offering wine and spirits would remain.

"A baby," Lydia said.

CHAPTER 3

❄

DECEMBER 25, 1813

Lydia was vaguely aware of knocking and of her name being called.

"Are you ready, love?" Miles asked through the door. "You know how my mother despises when anyone is late."

Lydia said nothing. Her chest rose and fell in a freshly laundered chemise, and she stared blankly at the dirty one in her hands. She had shed it in such a hurry, eager to dress for Christmas dinner, that she hadn't noticed the stain until she had picked it up to set it where her maid would notice and take it to be washed.

The door opened. "Lydia?" Miles walked in. "I thought you would be dressed by—" He stopped in his tracks, and without even glancing at him, she knew he was looking at the fabric in her hands and the large patch of crimson that stared back at her like an abyss.

A tear slipped from Lydia's eye, and she made no effort to brush it away, not even blinking.

"Is that—?"

She didn't respond. If she didn't say it, perhaps it wouldn't be real.

Miles stayed where he was for a moment then came over to settle in beside her, wrapping an arm about her. They sat in silence together, and soon the blood on the chemise was joined by tear drops.

❆

The Present

Lydia had doubted the noise at first. She had woken in the nighttime more than once to baby cries, only to realize that they had been part of a dream, nothing more. She wondered if perhaps she was hearing such cries during her waking hours as well now.

But then the dowager baroness had said something.

Her mother-in-law approached the nativity, and Lydia broke her arm away from Miles's to follow, heading straight for the manger, where the blanket seemed to be moving.

"Good heavens," said the dowager baroness, as Lydia came up beside her.

Lydia crouched down beside the manger, pulling the blanket from the baby's face—the reason for its muffled cries. Below the blanket there was no clothing, only the baby's smooth and milky skin.

Its cries increased, and Lydia hurried to tuck the blanket back around the exposed skin.

Miles knelt down next to her. "Poor chap," he said.

"Or girl," Lydia said, looking around them for any sign of a mother or father—even an older sibling.

"I thought it was a doll here before," said the dowager baroness, speaking more loudly than usual over the heightening cries of the babe.

"It was." Lydia said, and she scooped her hands beneath the baby and lifted it out of the manger. Bits of straw clung to the blanket it was in. Certainly not a warm enough blanket for the cold of the night surrounding them. Where was the babe's mother?

She stared down into the infant's face, with its watering eyes and red nose.

"My dear," said Miles, glancing around them. "Perhaps we should…"

Lydia unbuttoned her pelisse with one hand and slipped the baby inside, arranging the blanket around it. "We cannot leave her to freeze." The baby's cries began to abate. "Shh. Shh. There, there, little one."

"Surely the mother has only gone to fetch the cart or some such errand," said the dowager baroness, looking all around. But the area around the nativity was nearly deserted. Above them, the hum of voices and the drum of footsteps sounded as people walked across the bridge.

Diana came up to Lydia and peeked in her pelisse. "What a sweet little thing."

"I shall go ask if anyone has seen the mother," said Miles, and with quick steps, he approached the nearest merchant.

"I can help," Diana said, setting her mug down next to the manger. Mary nodded, following her sister in the opposite direction as Miles.

Lydia watched as Miles approached the nearest merchant and conversed with him. The man frowned and glanced over at Lydia and the dowager baroness, shaking his head.

She looked down at the baby in her arms, fussing a bit but no longer crying out as before. The body was warm against hers, and she stifled an impulse to nuzzle her nose against the rosy cheeks. "Where is your mother, my dear?" she asked in a whisper.

"I certainly hope it hasn't been abandoned," said the dowager baroness. "What a terrible night to do such a thing."

Lydia's throat constricted, and she stifled her response. What night *wouldn't* be a terrible one on which to abandon a helpless babe? At least here there were people to take notice. But how could anyone abandon an innocent baby like the darling one she held? She knew that there were many women less fortunate than she, but it seemed so terribly unfair that someone who wanted a baby more than anything in the world could not have one no matter what she tried, while others were desperate enough to desert theirs.

Miles came up beside her. "He says he hasn't seen anyone here for nigh on an hour."

Diana and Mary returned shortly after, shaking their heads. "No one has any information to offer. They said the people left here some time ago, though."

"Perhaps we should find a constable," said the dowager baroness. "I have seen a few about. They will know what to do."

"Don't fret," said Lydia to the baby, looking around again as though they might suddenly see the mother walking toward them. She was hesitant to take the baby from the place she had been left, but surely it would be better to do something than nothing. The sweet child couldn't be more than a few months old. "We shall ensure you are cared for. We shan't leave you." She looked up to see Miles's eyes upon her, though she wasn't certain what the sentiment there was.

The mugs were taken up again, and the group made their way toward the north bank of the river, everyone's eyes searching for a constable. The feeling at the fair had shifted distinctly toward one of a more rowdy nature, with men laughing raucously inside many of the fuddling tents where gin was being sold. It was certainly no place for a baby, nor a genteel woman, for that matter.

"There!" said Diana, pointing to a man with a club hanging from his side. He was looking down at another man sprawled on the ground, a tankard of spilled spirits in hand as he tried sluggishly to push himself up.

They hurried over to him, and Lydia brought up the rear, walking as carefully as she could with such a precious bundle in her charge. Miles noticed her lagging behind and fell back. "Would you like me to carry him?"

She shook her head. It was selfish, perhaps, but she didn't know how long it would be until she held a baby in her arms again. The infant fit there so perfectly.

The constable had the man before him by the collar of his coat. "I'll not have any more brawling," he said, and the man chuckled lazily.

Lydia slowed her walk, not wishing to get any closer to the drunken man, but Miles continued to the constable.

"Excuse me, sir," Miles said, and the constable glanced at him quickly before returning his eyes to the drunkard. "We've found an infant. It seems to have been abandoned."

The inebriated man was looking at the constable with a gaze equal parts muddled and challenging, and he tossed a punch into the air at nothing and no one in particular, snorting with laughter and raising his tankard to his lips, only to draw it away again with a frown as he realized it was empty.

The constable was anything but amused. "You can set the baby down over there." He motioned carelessly toward somewhere to his side, never letting his gaze stray from the drunkard.

Lydia followed the direction of the constable's gesture. There was nothing but ice there, being traipsed over by other inebriated men who hadn't a care what was below them, evidenced by one of them tripping over an uneven bit of ground. She looked at Miles, who wore an expression of displeasure.

"We cannot simply leave the baby on the ground, sir," he said. "It would be better off in the manger where we found it."

The constable turned toward him with a brittle smile and made a showy gesture. "Then, by all means, return it there."

The drunken man tossed his tankard onto the ice, and Lydia instinctively stepped back, drawing the baby closer to her. She was beginning to fuss again.

Miles grimaced. "If you could just tell us where you intend to take the infant after dealing with...matters, we can take him there ourselves."

"He'll go to the workhouse," said the constable.

Lydia's heart dropped. An innocent baby to the workhouse? She looked at Miles, who looked nearly as horrified as she felt.

"The workhouse?" he said.

The constable didn't even answer. He was busy wrestling the drunk man.

Seeming to understand he wasn't going to receive any more information, Miles came over to Lydia, pulling the blanket to the side with a finger to look down at the baby, who was wriggling and upset.

"I wonder if she's hungry," Lydia said.

The dowager baroness came over to peer down at the infant as well. "Perhaps so. It looks to be old enough that it might already be weaned. Very near to six months old, I think."

"What should we do?" Miles asked no one in particular.

Lydia already knew what they should do, but she hesitated to say it. "Well, we cannot leave her here. I would be surprised if the constable even remembered."

The dowager baroness looked up at her with a measuring look. "What, then, do you suggest? You cannot take the poor thing with you."

Lydia swallowed. "What other option is there? It is late and frigidly cold. What the baby needs is a warm place to sleep and some food. We can easily provide that. Can't we?" She looked at Miles beside her.

He nodded. "It is clear nothing will be done for the infant anytime soon, Mother. You heard the constable."

The dowager baroness pursed her lips. "I suppose you are right. More can be done for the poor thing tomorrow."

Lydia let out a controlled sigh of relief. Her mother in law wasn't heartless by any means, but she could be quite rigid in her notions of what was proper.

"Well, then," Diana said, "shall we press on to find the coach? It will be warmer there. And we still need to return these mugs." She lifted the ones in her hands.

The baby's cries increased, and Lydia bounced as she shushed. "Is there any at all left? Of the hot chocolate?"

Diana peered into the mugs and grimaced. "There are a few drops left in this one." She cocked a brow at Mary. "You know how Mary never *quite* finishes anything she eats or drinks."

Mary smiled guiltily, and Miles took the mug from her. He hesitated for a moment, seemingly unsure about how to get the little remaining liquid into the baby's mouth.

"Perhaps you could just put a bit on your finger," Lydia suggested. "Just to see if she likes it."

Miles removed a glove and obediently dipped his finger into the mug, transferring it to the infant's mouth. The crying ceased as the baby sucked on Miles's forefinger, eyes closing and a few declining whimpers coming from her. Lydia met eyes with Miles, and they both smiled at the sweet sounds.

"Ow!" Miles snatched his hand away and looked at his finger. "He bit me!"

Lydia pulled in her lips to stifle a laugh. "I imagine she wants more."

Miles's brows contracted, and he sent the baby a glower. "Funny way of showing it." He dipped his finger back in the hot chocolate and, with a bit of hesitation, offered it to the infant again. He allowed a few sucks before pulling his finger away, a victorious smile stretching across his lips. "Ha!" he said, and he dipped his finger again.

The hot chocolate was soon gone, but the baby seemed to be satiated enough that she had managed to fall asleep, and Lydia's heart both swelled and ached at the sight of the peaceful sight—long, crescent lashes on full cheeks, with a bottom lip that pouted slightly.

They made their way back to the north side of the bridge, where Mary and Diana returned the mugs. Thanks to the dispersal of the crowds while they had been occupied with the baby, they found that the coach driver had managed to bring the equipage to the same place he had left them hours ago.

All eyes were on the bundle in Lydia's arms, quiet and calm, once the group was seated in the carriage. But the first jostling of the coach seemed to rouse the babe, who blinked up at Lydia for a time then wriggled. She managed to wrest an arm free after a moment then reached up to Lydia's bonnet ribbons. It took a moment for her to close her fingers around the ribbon, and Lydia glanced up with a smile at Miles, who watched in amusement.

A sudden tug yanked Lydia's head down. "Oh!" she cried in surprise, and laughs filled the coach.

"He's much stronger than he looks," Miles said, helping to unfurl the baby's fingers from the ribbon.

"Perhaps I should just remove my bonnet," Lydia said. "Would you...?" She held out her arms toward Miles, and he paused briefly before slipping his hands beneath the baby.

"Yes," Lydia said, transferring the bundle to him. "Just support her head."

Miles's shoulders were tense and high, but as he settled back into the squabs, they relaxed a bit, and a soft smile pulled at his lips.

Lydia watched with another little ache in her heart. Seeing him hold a baby brought another layer of hurt to their own lack. She untied her ribbons and pulled the bonnet from her head, setting it beside her, but she let Miles hold the baby for a while longer. Heaven only knew when she would see such a sight again.

Miles was meant to be a father, and Lydia despaired that he ever would be one.

CHAPTER 4

MARCH 1814

A gust of spring wind blew through the open window of Miles's bedchamber, followed by a slight creaking. He glanced toward the sound as he straightened his cravat, and his hands stilled.

The cradle beside the bed—Lydia's side of the bed—swayed gently, the creaking getting more faint as it slowed then stopped altogether.

He tightened his jaw against the feelings that the sight brought. He was a fool for keeping it there as long as he had. He should have removed it as soon as it became apparent that Lydia wasn't coming back to share his bed.

It represented a silly hope. There was no baby to sleep in the cradle. And, even if there had been hope of a baby after all these years of trying, there was no prospect of realizing such a hope when his wife kept far away from him. It had been nearly six months since they'd shared a bed.

She had given up. And he couldn't blame her. Somehow, somewhere along the line, their intimacy had come to feel somewhat like a chore.

He stared at the crib a moment longer then stepped decisively toward the bell pull and tugged it. It was time for the crib to go elsewhere.

❄

The Present

For years, Miles had thought of having a child in terms of the heir he would raise up to take his place—a young man in need of guidance and apprenticeship.

Somehow he had never considered the years leading up to that—what it would feel like to hold a baby in his arms. The warmth against his chest, the weight of the baby both grounding him and pressing upon him with the significance of the life he held. This baby was not his—not bone of his bone or flesh of his flesh—but just now, it relied upon him for survival. Its future was in his hands in a very real sense.

Even if he hadn't agreed with Lydia that they should bring the baby home with them, he didn't know if he would have been able to nay-say his wife. He had seen in her eyes what she wanted, even if she hadn't had the courage to say it aloud.

She was meant to be a mother—to help and serve and teach and nurture. And even if she'd had four of her own children at her feet, she wouldn't have been able to turn away a child in need.

The coach rolled to a stop in front of his mother's townhouse, and she looked at the baby with a slight softening of the eyes as he made cooing noises and tugged on Miles's cravat.

"Don't let the child keep you up until all hours of the night," she said. "Jane will know how to care for it."

Miles nodded. "Goodnight, Mother."

When they arrived at the Lynham townhouse a few minutes later, Miles handed the baby to Lydia as he descended from the carriage and helped the three women down. They all went up the steps and into the house with a great yawn from Diana, followed quickly by one from Mary.

"I am for bed," Diana said. She smiled sweetly and lightly ruffled the baby's sparse, brown hair. "Goodnight, little ragamuffin."

"He is *not* a ragamuffin," Mary said, pinching the baby's ample cheek. She glanced at Lydia hurriedly. "Or she, rather."

Lydia laughed, and Miles relished in the sound as Diana and Mary went up the stairs and disappeared toward their shared bedchamber.

The baby was chomping on his own hand, which was wet with slobber, so much so that a stream of it dripped onto Lydia's pelisse. She only smiled and said, "Let us get you something a bit more filling to eat, shall we?"

"I'll call for Jane," Miles said, going to tug the bell cord.

"No," Lydia said. "You needn't bother. I shall take her to Jane myself."

Miles shrugged. "Very well."

Lydia pulled the baby's hand from his mouth and jostled it around. "I just want to be sure Jane knows what she needs."

Miles took a step closer and lowered his head until the baby's gaze found his. "Goodnight, little chap." The baby's mouth pulled into a wide, open-mouthed smile, and he set a slobbery hand on Miles's face.

Lydia let out an ill-stifled laugh, and Miles couldn't stop his own smile.

"You intend to put me in my place, don't you?" he said to the baby, who cooed.

Miles wiped at his face with a handkerchief then hesitated for a moment, wondering if he might slip a kiss onto Lydia's cheek while she was in such high spirits. Why did the thought of such a small gesture make his heart pound so violently?

He ducked in and kissed her cheek lightly. "Goodnight, my dear."

"Goodnight, Miles," she said, gaze still on the baby. It was much better than the wary look that usually entered her eyes when he attempted such things. A small success.

With the help of his valet, Miles undressed, his mind consumed with the strange events of the night. He hardly knew what to think of it all.

He tossed and turned in his bed, unable to scrub from his thoughts the picture of Lydia holding the baby, as if it was the most precious thing on the planet. He drifted off to sleep a few times, only to wake with a start after restless dreams of the Frost Fair and bundled babies left on the ice.

He scrubbed a hand over his tired eyes and picked up his pocket watch from the bedside table. It was nearly one in the morning. He often woke in the middle of the night. Sleep had never come quite as easily to him since he and Lydia had stopped sharing a bed. He would never tell her as much, but sometimes, when he found it particularly hard to sleep, he would check on her in her room, watching the rise and fall of her chest for just a moment from the door to her bedchamber. He missed the sight of her sleeping beside him, though truthfully, he wasn't sure if his nighttime expeditions were more helpful or hurtful to his heart.

He listened for any signs of a baby cry, but the house was still. How was the baby faring? Had Jane managed to get him to sleep? *Was* it a him?

He lay in bed for a few more minutes, but sleep evaded him, and finally, he swung his legs over the side of the bed. He would just make sure that the entire house was asleep, the baby included. Using the fire in his grate, he lit a candle and made his way down the stairs.

All the lights were out in the kitchen—and everywhere, really. Hopefully the babe was sleeping soundly in the small cradle they had been storing downstairs. He made his way back up to his bedchamber, stopping in the corridor in front of his door, gaze trained on the door farther down the hall.

He shouldn't. He should just go back to his own bed. But he couldn't help himself.

He stepped gently up to the door of his wife's bedchamber and stopped. "You're a fool, Miles," he said softly, but he lifted the latch anyway and opened the door just enough to see into the dark room, lit only by the fire.

Lydia was fast asleep, on her right side, and with a hand resting under her head. She always slept the same way. His heart twinged. She was much more peaceful than usual.

He sighed then squinted, opening the door a bit wider to better see the small heap of linens next to the bed. It wasn't like Sarah to leave things in disorder.

But it wasn't a heap of linens. It was the cradle.

There was a slight stirring in the blankets within then stillness again.

He swallowed.

For so long now, he and Lydia had parted ways at night. His only consolation was that Lydia's room had been just as empty as his. Tonight, though, she slept with a baby beside her—what she had been wanting all along.

She had loved him when they had married. He never doubted that. But over the course of the past few years, her desires had changed. Never had he felt more keenly that she didn't need him, and it was a stab in the most tender part of his heart.

He shut the door to his wife's bedchamber softly and sighed, turning back toward his own empty room.

CHAPTER 5

JANUARY 1810

Miles's man of business, Mr. Hindley, opened the door of the London townhouse with an old, brass key, pushing the door wide to make room for Miles and Lydia. She glanced around the entry hall. It was a bit narrower than the last but certainly not lacking in beauty. It was cold inside—only marginally warmer than the January air they were coming in from. She tried to imagine how it would feel with fires warming each and every hearth.

"This one," said Hindley, "was owned by Sir John Birchworth. He purchased it nearly two years ago and immediately went to work on the furnishings. Unfortunately, his zeal acquired him many debts, and he is now obliged to sell it in order to rein in his expenses."

"His loss may well be our gain." Miles winked at Lydia then took her hand in his.

Hindley led them through the house, conveying what information he had received from Sir John. When they had gone through all the rooms, he left Lydia and Miles alone to discuss things.

"What do you think?" Miles asked. "It is certainly larger than the last two we saw. And a bit more expensive. Closer to my mother, as well."

Lydia nodded. "It is larger, but that is not a bad thing necessarily. Plenty of room to grow into." She averted her gaze. They had been married for only two weeks, and she was still accustoming herself to speaking of such things.

"Very true," he said with an enigmatic smile, and he wrapped an arm about her waist, pulling her toward him. "Add in a few children, and this place will feel full to the brim."

She went up on her tiptoes and closed her eyes, delighting in the feel of his lips on hers and the security of his arms around her.

"On second thought," Miles said, letting their foreheads rest against each other, "I am not entirely certain I am ready to give up all my alone time with you just yet."

She laughed softly, playing with a button on his waistcoat. "Do you wish to wait to start our family?" *Our family*. The very words warmed her.

"No," he said, and he pulled away, glancing toward the window. "I can see it now. A crib right there"—he pointed to the space between the four-poster bed and the window—"and little Matthew running through the corridor, being chased after by his nurse."

"Matthew?"

He looked at her. "Do you like it? I have always liked that name."

"I love it," she said. Knowing that he had been thinking of names for their children made her love him all the more.

It was easy to envision this as the home she would share with Miles and their children—the setting for fond memories for years to come. They would spend much of the year at Lynham Place, of course, but in Town...yes, this could be home away from home.

❄

The Present

Lydia's eyelids fluttered for a moment, the sounds of her dream lingering in the form of baby coos. She let her eyes remain closed, knowing from plenty of experience that the wisps of dream were impossible to grasp at this point.

But the coos grew louder.

Her eyes flew open, and she whipped her head to the side, memories flitting back through her mind as her gaze fell on the chubby little arms reaching up from the cradle beside her bed.

Her heart stopped then thudded like a drum against her ribs. She whipped the bedcovers over and hurried to crouch beside the cradle.

The baby's eyes latched onto her and his mouth—it had become clear the night before while changing a soiled nappy that the baby was indeed a *he*—stretched slowly into a smile.

"Good morning, you sweet thing," Lydia said as she reached into the cradle. She had never awoken to a more welcome sight. Certainly not since sleeping alone, at least. Her eyes were heavy. It had taken some time—and a great deal of rocking and singing—for the baby to settle and fall asleep, and he had woken hungry once during the night. He was in a new place entirely, and she wanted to ensure he felt safe.

"Shall we get you something to eat? What do you say? I just need to change first. Not all of us can wear naught but a blanket and feel presentable." They would need to get the babe some proper clothing somehow.

She tugged on the bell and took the baby over to the window while they awaited her maid. The cold air from outside brought a chill inside, and she held him closer, but he leaned forward toward the window, setting his plump fingers upon it.

Sarah came in, and Lydia set the baby back in the cradle as she dressed for the day, keeping an amused eye on him. He was entranced by the molding work on the ceiling.

When Sarah left, Lydia took the boy back in her arms, allowing him to hold her finger tightly in his grasp. She let out a sigh, feeling a reluctance to leave the room. It felt like a little slice of a dream there, tired as she felt. And when she left the haven, she knew what would come next: a discussion of what to do with the baby. But it couldn't be put off forever.

Miles was partaking of breakfast in the dining room—Diana and Mary were absent, as Lydia had expected based on the habit they had acquired since being in Town of staying abed late—and he looked up at the opening of the door, pushing his chair out from the table with a smile.

"And how is this little man doing?"

Lydia smiled, wondering if Miles knew she had let the baby sleep in her room. He could have easily discovered as much from the servants.

"Did he let you get any rest?" Miles tapped the baby on the nose lightly then looked at Lydia. He knew.

She smiled sheepishly. "Yes, he did. After nine lullabies and a fair amount of bouncing, we came to an understanding."

"Spoiled rotten is what you were, then," he said without animus. "I can hold him while you eat."

"Oh, no. You finish first. I didn't mean to disturb your meal."

He shrugged. "I'm nearly done," he said, and he pulled the babe from her arms. "He can sit on my lap while I finish."

"Thank you, Miles," she said. She *was* starving. "Jane should be here with a bottle for him soon, but based on last night, it seems he's quite interested in other types of food as well."

They sat down at the table, and Lydia glanced at Miles arranging the baby on his lap, comfortably reclined in the crook of his left arm. She couldn't help but feel the bittersweetness of it. It was like a picture out of the life they had planned together. The life that had never been realized. And never would be.

She put aside her melancholy thoughts as she reached for a roll—it was impossible not to smile at the picture Miles and the baby presented. He had left his reclined position in favor of the more thrilling prospect of the remaining food on Miles's plate. Over and over again, Miles pulled the infant's hands back where they belonged, but the baby was determined and began to fuss slightly.

"You're a persistent chap, aren't you?" Miles pushed the plate farther away. "Here." He pulled a piece from the last bite of toast remaining.

"Oh, not too much, Miles," Lydia said nervously.

He obediently broke it into a smaller portion and put it up against the baby's lips. The baby shoved the bread into his mouth energetically, smacking his lips as he tried to decide what to do with it.

Miles and Lydia both laughed, and their gazes met. He nodded at her food. "You haven't eaten anything."

Her tea and roll were untouched, and she reached for a knife, scooping preserves from the nearby jar. "You two are too entertaining."

Miles's gaze shifted to the baby, and he sighed. "What are we going to do with you, child?"

Lydia's smile disappeared, and she focused on spreading the preserves.

"I've been thinking," he said. "What about the Foundling Hospital?"

Lydia's hand slowed. "The Foundling Hospital?" She looked up in time to see Miles grab a fork from the baby's hand.

"Yes," he said. "It certainly seems preferable to the alternative the constable mentioned."

"Is it?" she asked. She had heard of the Foundling Hospital, but that was the extent of her knowledge.

"Do you not agree? Its entire purpose is to provide for foundlings."

Lydia looked at the baby. He was a veritable cherub, and she felt the urge to hold him in her arms once again. It was silly to feel an attachment to a stranger's child—one she had only known for a handful of hours. And yet feel it she did.

"Certainly it is preferable to the workhouse, but I don't know, Miles." Her heart pattered against her chest as she tried to decide whether to make a different suggestion. If she didn't say it now, she would always regret it. "Is there a reason *we* can't keep him?"

Miles's brows drew together in a look of something uncomfortably near to pity, and heat crept into Lydia's cheeks.

"Lydia." He sighed and reached a hand toward her. "What if his mother comes to look for him? It may be unlikely, but it *is* a possibility, and surely she is most likely to look for him at the parish or the Foundling Hospital. You must see we cannot keep the chap. He isn't *ours* to keep."

Lydia tried for a smile. The baby wasn't theirs, but that was just it, wasn't it? What baby ever would be?

She tried to picture what the baby's mother might be like. *Would* she come looking for him? Did she regret leaving him there in the cold, with naught but a blanket? It was the act of a desperate woman. Perhaps she had spent a sleepless night, wondering about her child.

"What sort of a place is it?" Lydia asked with a lump in her throat. "The Foundling Hospital, I mean."

The baby started fussing, as if he knew what they were speaking of, and Miles bounced his knee up and down rhythmically. "I can't say. I've only ever seen the outside. It looks to be a nice enough place. Perhaps we should go see for ourselves. If we find it acceptable, we can leave him there. If not...." He didn't finish.

Lydia swallowed. It was a perfectly rational suggestion. "Very well."

❄

The gate opened, and the coach tumbled over the cobblestone and into the wide expanse that led up to the Foundling Hospital. Lydia let the baby stare through the coach window, wide-eyed. He had likely never been in a coach until last night. It was a new way of seeing the world, and it made it feel new for Lydia too.

The coachman let them down in front of the central building at the far end of the courtyard, and Miles helped Lydia from the carriage. It was as cold as it had been the day before, and Lydia readjusted the baby's blankets. A queue of girls led by a severe woman in subdued clothing emerged from a doorway adjacent to the center building. They wore brown serge dresses with white aprons and caps, and each one held a book in her hand as she walked in concert with her fellows, all wearing serious expressions, their breath puffing before them in small white clouds.

"Come, my dear." Miles was opening the door for her, and Lydia followed him inside where, after a few minutes, they were greeted by a somewhat harried man.

"Good day," he said, eyes flicking toward the baby.

Miles put his hand on Lydia's back. "My name is Lord Lynham, and this is my wife, Lady Lynham."

The man gave a quick bow, one of his brows quirking upward in surprise. "Pleased to make your acquaintances. I am Robert Moss, and I am Secretary of the hospital. How can I assist you?"

"We had a few questions for you about the hospital."

"I will do my best to answer them, my lord." His eyes flitted down the corridor behind Lydia and Miles.

Miles nodded at Lydia.

She bounced gently. The baby's eyelids seemed to be growing heavy, though he appeared to be fighting the desire to sleep, too interested in the people and surroundings to submit to such a boring activity. "I am afraid I am sadly ignorant," she said. "What exactly *do* you do with the babies here at the hospital when they arrive?"

Mr. Moss clasped his hands in front of him and straightened. She had the impression this was not his first time being asked the question. "Each baby is baptized and given a new name shortly after arrival. After that, they are sent to the country to a nurse, who cares for them until their return when they are four or five years old."

"Oh," Lydia said. She had assumed that the babies were cared for right at the hospital. But perhaps it was better that they experience the beginnings of childhood in a place with more fresh air and room to play than they would have in Town. "And once they return?"

"They are inoculated against smallpox directly upon arrival then educated and prepared to become apprentices and servants over the next few years. Most of them begin some sort of apprenticeship when they turn fourteen."

It was a good answer, really. While the life of a servant was certainly not what she would wish for her own children, it was a far cry better than what a child would experience growing up in the workhouse.

She glanced at Miles. He was watching her, no doubt wondering how she felt about what they were hearing. They held one another's gaze for a moment then he turned back to Mr. Moss. "We happened upon this baby"—he nodded toward him—"last night while at the Frost Fair, seemingly abandoned in a nativity display that had been put on by what appeared to be a group of Irish Catholics. It was quite late when we discovered him there, crying, and none of the nearby merchants were able to provide any information about who might have left the child there. Given the circumstances, we thought it best to take him home with us until we could decide upon the best course of action, which brings us here."

Mr. Moss's lips were pulled into a thin line. "I am afraid you have come for little purpose, then."

Lydia's soft swaying slowed, and she looked at her husband, whose brow was furrowed.

"I am sorry," Miles said. "I don't understand."

"We have a strict admittance process, my lord," said Mr. Moss. "We are only at liberty to accept babies who are brought by their own mothers, and even then, there is a procedure in place."

"But...but...it is a foundling hospital. How can you not accept foundlings?"

He grimaced. "We have had to adjust the way we operate over the years, I'm afraid. All babies were accepted at one point. At other times, foundlings with a donation of £100 were accepted. But at this time, we can only accept babies under the age of twelve months who have been born out of wedlock to a first-time mother in distress—and intent upon returning to the Lord through repentance."

There was an uncomfortable moment of silence. "Then what is to become of babies like this one?"

The baby was sound asleep now, his bottom lip jutting out in a lovable pout.

Mr. Moss shrugged apologetically. "They are the responsibility of the parish."

"So, it is the workhouse for them."

Mr. Moss nodded slowly. "I wish I could tell you differently, but it is not my decision, unfortunately. We cannot possibly take on *all* the orphaned children in this town. Particularly at such a time as this. We have had three mothers come in just this morning. Cold winters are not kind to the poor."

"I can imagine," Miles said. "Might we leave our names with you, then? Should the mother happen to come here in search of the baby, I mean. That way you could send us a message."

He nodded. "I have your names. Lord and Lady Lynham, was it not? I will make note of them in the office."

Someone appeared in a doorway down the corridor and motioned to Mr. Moss, who nodded and turned back to Lydia and Miles. "I apologize not to be of more help. It was very kind of you to take the infant in. And now, if you'll excuse me, I must finish the admission process for one of the newcomers. I wish you a good day, my lord. My lady." He bowed and, with a quick stride, disappeared down the corridor and through a door.

Lydia looked at Miles, unable to dispel the sick feeling lodged in the pit of her stomach.

"Come," he said, brows drawn together. "There is nothing for us here."

The coach was brought back around, and they stepped up into it. Lydia couldn't help but feel relieved that she wasn't obliged to leave the baby at the hospital. It wasn't only that she didn't wish to say goodbye, though she certainly didn't.

There was nothing ominous in the picture she had seen of the girls lined up and walking across the courtyard, but it had affected her all the same. What must it be like to grow up in such a place? With teachers and fellow orphans but no mother or father? To wonder if you would ever live to see the face of the woman who bore you?

She looked at the babe in her arms. She didn't know if she could have subjected him to such a future, little as she knew him. Did he not deserve more? Did not every child?

Miles let out a frustrated sigh. "Well, that was certainly not what I had expected."

"No," said Lydia. She was scared to ask, but she couldn't make herself wait a moment longer. "What now?"

Miles tapped a finger on the top hat in his lap. "I hardly know." He looked out of the window thoughtfully.

Lydia's heart thudded against her chest, and the only sound was the rumbling of the coach wheels. "Might we not keep him?"

Miles's head whipped around toward her.

"Just for a while. Until we decide what is best done. We cannot leave him at the mercy of the parish, Miles."

"No," he agreed, eyes on the babe.

Lydia shrugged, hoping she seemed more nonchalant than she felt. "We could keep him with us during Christmastide. It is so terribly cold, and with Christmas only two days away, I imagine it would be difficult to do anything else. People are taken up with preparing Christmas dinner and that sort of thing. We could give him a proper experience of the season, just as we plan to do with Diana and Mary."

Miles said nothing, still staring thoughtfully at the baby. "Yes, I suppose you're right." He looked up at Lydia, and he smiled. "Let's keep him with us while we try to arrange for a proper situation. I'm sure we can find something by Epiphany."

Lydia nodded quickly, unable to keep from smiling. Epiphany was still more than a fortnight away. "Yes, yes, of course."

Miles came to sit beside her and peered down at the baby. "He *is* a handsome little chap, isn't he?"

"He is. Do you intend to keep calling him *little chap* for the next two weeks? Perhaps we should decide upon a name for him—I find it somewhat awkward to keep referring to him as *the baby*."

Miles chuckled and pushed a tuft of the baby's hair aside. "Yes, I think he should have some sort of name. They would have given him one at the Foundling Hospital, after all. But what name?"

"What about Matthew?" She chanced a glance at Miles, whose gaze flew to hers.

He opened his mouth then shut it.

"You dislike the idea?" she asked.

He looked reluctant to respond. "It is just...that is the name I was hoping to use for...."

Lydia nodded quickly even as her heart plummeted. "Oh, yes. I had forgotten." It wasn't true. She hadn't forgotten. It was the name he had spoken of so many years ago—what felt like a lifetime, really—when they had planned for their future with all the confidence of a young couple in love, certain that what lay before them was every bit as promising as the present.

But much had happened since then. And she had hoped he had become resigned to the fact that they would never conceive a child together. Clearly, that was not the case, and the knowledge settled heavily upon her.

"What about Thomas?" he suggested.

Lydia mustered a smile and a nod. "Yes, Thomas."

CHAPTER 6

❄

JANUARY 1814

Miles reached an arm out and wrapped it around his wife's waist, setting a kiss on the soft skin of her upper arm.

There was no response to his gesture, and he pushed himself up on his elbow to see whether she was already asleep. Her ability to fall asleep quickly seemed to have increased dramatically of late. It used to take her half an hour to wind down at night, a time often filled with talk of the day as Miles struggled to stay awake enough to offer coherent responses.

Not so anymore.

Her eyes were closed, but her breathing hadn't slowed or deepened, and he pulled her gently toward him, letting his lips seek out her neck. She smelled of violets, and he inhaled it slowly. "My love?"

She stirred slightly. "Not tonight, Miles."

He stilled, feeling the familiar hurt wrap around his heart like tentacles ready to crush it. He had only wanted to hold her closer—to talk to her about something besides the mundane things they spoke of day in, day out. But she always insisted on reading more into his affection.

"Not tonight," he repeated, releasing her from his hold and dropping back on his pillow. "Nor indeed any night." He didn't even know if she heard that last part, but it was true.

She turned toward him in bed, coming up on her elbow and looking at him with a flash of anger in her eyes. "What am I to understand from that?"

He lifted his shoulders. "There is always some excuse, isn't there?"

Her brows contracted, and he felt himself on dangerous ground. But he had gone for months without mentioning anything, much as it had been hurting him inside, and he didn't think he could keep silent any longer.

"You are always too tired or have the headache or have...."

She blinked at him. "Or have what?"

He pinched his lips together and sat up, debating whether he should say something. "Just the other night you told me you had started your courses."

Her eyes took on a wary look, but she said nothing.

"You aren't due to start your courses for another week at least, Lydia."

She drew back. "You keep such close track, then? An expert on the matter, in fact."

He said nothing. It wasn't terribly difficult to keep track, honestly. Not only were her courses very regular, he always noted a slight shift in her moods as they approached. He let out a sigh. He didn't want to fight with Lydia. He wanted to hold her. "I just fail to see what the purpose is of sharing a bed if we never speak here, let alone touch."

She was stiff—clearly on the defensive. "The purpose of a bed is to have a place to sleep, is it not?"

"Yes, of course, but...it used to be more than that."

"Yes," she said with more passion than she usually displayed. "And look what we have to show for it—nothing at all!" She pushed the bedcovers back and slipped out of bed. "I cannot do this anymore,

Miles—pretend that something is suddenly going to change when it has been the same these four years."

Her words implied that the only purpose to their intimacy was that of producing an heir. He wanted an heir, of course. Desperately. But what he shared with his wife was so much more than that. Was that all it was to her?

"Well, it certainly isn't going to change if you are unwilling to keep trying—if you won't let me so much as touch you," Miles said, and he could hear the irritation and hurt in his own voice.

She swallowed hard and took a step back. "Perhaps you are right. There is little purpose to sharing a bed at this point. Goodnight, Miles." She turned away and, in a few long strides, was gone from the room.

❄

The Present

Miles had been hesitant to agree to Lydia's suggestion to keep the baby with them for the time being. He could see it in her eyes—the way they pleaded with him, the way they softened every time she looked at Thomas. He didn't know what to think of it. Was it good for her? Or was he setting her up for heartache when Thomas left?

But he couldn't see an alternative—at least one that didn't involve leaving the baby with the parish. And Lydia was right. They couldn't do that—subjecting a young, innocent baby to the squalor and the hardships of such a life. Such things happened, of course, but there was a difference between it happening unbeknownst to them and taking the baby there themselves. There had to be a better option, but it would take time to search it out.

Upon discovering that Thomas was to stay, Diana and Mary were thrilled. Diana took the baby in her arms and danced around the room with him. He was doted upon by all three women, but there was something different in the attention paid Thomas by Lydia. It was motherly—responsible and watchful, even when she smiled at her sisters' antics with the child, as if she was ready to step in and call for them to take greater care if it became needed.

When it came time for sleep, Miles was grateful when Mary asked Lydia if she meant to hand the baby off to one of the servants. He wasn't the only one who thought it the best arrangement.

"Oh, no," Lydia said. "I am quite happy to have him sleep by me. He did better than expected last night, and I imagine he will do even better tonight."

"And what of you, Miles?" asked Diana. "Are you so content to have your sleep disturbed by this little urchin?" She rubbed her nose against Thomas's and was rewarded by his grabbing a handful of hair from her coiffure.

An awkward silence followed her question, but Diana was taken up with prying her hair loose and seemed not to notice. Miles *wouldn't* be disturbed by Thomas where he slept.

"He is not an urchin," Lydia said, pulling the baby from her sister with chastising brows but a teasing smile—one that faded slightly once she had turned her face from the view of her sisters. "Come, Thomas. Let us leave these unfeeling wretches and get you something to tide you over till morning." She sent a saucy but teasing look at her sisters then left the room.

Before any more could be said on the topic of how Thomas might affect his sleep, Miles begged leave of Diana and Mary. It was too early for him to turn in for the night, but he would find something to occupy him for the next hour if it meant avoiding an awkward topic of conversation. The last time the Donnely sisters had stayed with them, Lydia and Miles had been in their first year of marriage and so unashamed of their affection for one another that it boggled Miles to remember. Diana and Mary were well aware that Lydia and Miles had always shared a bedchamber, leaving the adjoining room—and the door that connected it to Miles's—locked due to its misuse. That was not the case anymore, though.

It was as Miles had a hand on the doorknob of his bedchamber that Diana appeared, hurrying toward him.

"Oh," she said. "There you are! Would you tell Lydia to come out here for a moment?" She was slightly breathless, and she waited expectantly, a piece of paper in hand.

He froze, his mind running a hundred miles an hour. She assumed that he could open the door and simply call to Lydia to come out. But she wasn't in the room.

"Yes, yes," he said. "Just a moment." He slipped into his bedchamber and closed the door behind him. It might seem strange to Diana, but that was preferable to the alternative. Lydia didn't wish her family to know of the heartache they were experiencing as they tried to bring a baby into the world. She disliked speaking of their infertility, and Miles certainly didn't wish her to be obliged to speak of it more than she already was. The merest acquaintances somehow felt it their privilege to inquire into the intimate details of Lydia and Miles's life.

He stepped over to the door that connected their bedchambers and knocked on it softly. Nothing.

He knocked a bit harder, and there was a pause and a fiddling of the lock before the door opened, revealing Lydia's confused—and wary—face. He knew that face. It was the one she wore when she feared he might ask her to share his bed. He hadn't seen it in months because he had stopped asking.

"Diana is outside my room," he said in a whisper. "She wishes to see you."

It took a moment for comprehension to dawn on Lydia's face, but dawn it did. "I see."

He made room for her to pass by, and she hurried into his room and toward the door, Thomas sitting contentedly in her arms. She disappeared into the corridor, and Miles stared after her with a frown. It was the first time she had been in his room in nigh on a year, fleeting as it had been. She would likely wait until Diana left and enter her bedchamber through its own door to avoid the inevitable encounter with Miles.

He tugged on the bell pull to summon his valet but shrugged off his coat and untied his cravat while he waited. The scent of violets had lingered behind Lydia, and it made the loneliness within him gape like the growing hole it was. He had hoped he would accustom himself to it, and in some ways he had. But there was always something to remind him of how things used to be. That was the tricky part of living in the same house with a person. There was no escaping such reminders.

He undid the button at his throat, and the door opened.

"Oh," Lydia said, stopping short with the door still ajar behind her. Her eyes flitted to his open shirt then back up to his face.

"I am sorry," he said. "I thought you would use the other door."

"No need to apologize," she said with a hurried smile. "I just didn't want Diana to..." She bit her lip nervously. She hadn't used to be so unsure of herself. Marriage to Miles had done that to her, and he hated himself for it.

He shook his head. "It's quite all right. Here." He strode over to the door between their bedchambers and opened it.

She came abreast of him and turned. "Would you like to say goodnight, Thomas?"

Thomas reached for Miles, finding purchase in the dangling collar of his shirt, which he yanked toward him, bringing Miles with it and up against Thomas and Lydia.

"Oh dear," Lydia said, pulling back a bit with a laugh. But there was nowhere for her to go.

Thomas's hands gripped the button on Miles's shirt, and Miles worked to wrest it from the baby's grasp, knowing that Lydia was likely uncomfortable with how near they were to one another, his lips close enough that they could brush her forehead if he wasn't careful.

He finally pried the chubby hand off the button and stepped away so that his back came up against the door frame. "Forgive me," he said on a shaky laugh.

Lydia looked up at him with twinkling eyes. "It's quite all right. He was very determined to have your button."

Miles relaxed a bit at her demeanor, allowing himself a smile. "I think he would have had it if I'd given him a moment longer." He glanced down and paused. A couple of threads hung from the tip of the collar, and the button was conspicuously absent.

Lydia grabbed Thomas's hand—poised at his mouth—and pulled it away with the type of laugh that Miles had always delighted in.

"It looks like he *did* manage to pull it off," Lydia said. She took the button and handed it back to Miles, looking up at him with a smile and her hair partially pulled out of its coiffure.

He put a couple of fingers to one of the more unkempt pieces. "Is this a creation of his as well?"

Her hand came up in a self-conscious motion and brushed against his.

"Yes," she said, tucking the hair behind her ear in a gesture Miles found adorable. "He seems to have an obsession with pulling on hair."

As if on cue, Thomas reached for her hair, and Miles stopped him, clucking his tongue. "If you wish to pull on someone's hair, you shall have to make do with your own—what little of it there is. Goodnight, Thomas." His gaze moved to Lydia, and he smiled at her. "If he bullies you too much, you need merely call for me."

Lydia smiled, and he wondered how long it had been since she had maintained eye contact with him for so long. He had begun to worry she was starting to fear him. "I promise you I shall."

"Goodnight, Lydia."

"Goodnight, Miles." She passed through to her own room, and he shut the door behind her, staying for a moment to listen to the muffled sounds of her speaking to Thomas until the door to his room opened to admit his valet Bailey.

CHAPTER 7

Christmas Eve dawned cloudy, gray, and just as cold as the days preceding it. Miles breakfasted early and left with one of the servants to seek out things they might use to decorate the house. He wanted to be certain Diana and Mary had an enjoyable time in Town, frigid as the weather might be.

When he returned well into the day, it was with two armfuls of greenery. As he and the servant discussed where to put it all, a head appeared in the doorway to the entry hall.

"Oh!" Diana said, coming toward them. "What a wonderful surprise! I thought it would be impossible to find anything like this given the state of the weather." She lifted a branch to her nose and shut her eyes. "It smells divine!"

Her admiration drew both Mary and Lydia into the entry hall, and Miles felt that perhaps all of the driving around Town in the freezing, ice covered streets might be worth it if only for the look of gratitude on his wife's face.

She mouthed the words *thank you* to him as both Mary and Diana discussed what the best places would be for draping the greenery. Everyone but Lydia filled their arms with it—hers were occupied with Thomas—and they made their way to the drawing room.

"And perhaps a kissing bough?" Diana said with an enigmatic look at Mary.

"To what purpose?" Mary asked. "I am more likely to pass under it while next to you than to happen beneath it in the company of a gentleman, aren't I? Or do we have a plan I am not aware of to host a bevy of eligible suitors?"

Miles grimaced. "The best we can plan for is perhaps my brother and one or two of his friends. I believe they are in Town, but Harry rarely informs me of his plans."

"Hm," said Mary. "Well, we can certainly make one just in case, but I imagine all the berries will be picked off by you and Lydia anyway."

Miles's gaze flew to Lydia, whose cheeks began to pink. She turned away from them and reached for a blanket draped over the nearest chair. "Diana, could you set that on the floor? I wish to lay Thomas down so I can use both hands to help with the decorating. Jane was kind enough to find this rattle while she was out yesterday, and I hope it will keep him occupied for a bit."

If Miles had harbored any hope that an encounter under the kissing bough would be welcomed by his wife, he would have added his voice to advocate for it. But it was more likely to cause awkwardness than anything else.

Diana laid the blanket down and smoothed it for Lydia to set Thomas upon it. As she rose from the floor, Diana looked at Miles through narrowed eyes and tilted her head to the side. "I have never met your brother, Miles. Is he as handsome as you?"

"Diana!" Lydia cried from her kneeling position.

Diana gave an innocent shrug. "What? You, of all people, would not deny that your husband is one of the most handsome men of our acquaintance."

Miles bit his lip to control a smile. He hadn't counted upon

Diana to make the case for him to his wife, but he was grateful for it, all the same.

"No," Lydia said, and her color was again heightened as she avoided Miles's eye, "but how very forward it makes you sound to ask such a question."

Miles cleared his throat. "I believe my brother is accounted by many to be the more handsome between us."

Diana's brows went up in an intrigued gesture. "Do you agree with that, Lydia?"

Lydia let out an incredulous breath and held the rattle in front of Thomas until he managed to grasp it. "You are incorrigible, Di."

"And *that* is not an answer to my question," she retorted. "Is it, Miles?"

Miles laughed. "Perhaps it is. She is afraid to hurt my feelings by telling the truth, but neither does she feel she can lie." He was rather enjoying himself. There had been little teasing between him and Lydia for some time, but given that Diana was orchestrating it, he couldn't pass up the opportunity.

Lydia primmed her lips together and stood. "Hardly. I am merely rising above the depths to which the conversation has sunk."

"Well," Diana said, "for my part, I am quite decided upon making a kissing bough, and I forbid the two of you"—she looked back and forth between Miles and Lydia—"from stealing all the berries before we know whether we shall be entertaining your brother and his friends or not. At least have the decency to do that."

Miles could think of nothing he would like more than to steal a great deal of kisses from Lydia under such a bough, but in the imagined scenario, his wife was a willing party, and that was not the reality of the situation.

"I have been wondering," Lydia said. "Do you think we might take something to the Foundling Hospital tomorrow? For the children. A little treat of some kind to brighten the day, perhaps. I haven't been able to put them from my mind since yesterday."

Of course she hadn't. It was one of the things he loved about her.

"It seems a very good idea to me. We can speak with Cook about it—see if she has any ideas."

Lydia smiled at him and nodded.

They had been stringing up garlands and folding paper flowers for an hour when the form of Miles's mother appeared in the doorway to the drawing room. She looked around, taking stock of the scene before her, which was a mess of half-hung greenery and stray remnants lying about the floor.

"Good heavens," she said with a smile. "What a scene you are to behold! Hello, Miss Donnely and Miss Mary."

The girls both offered a curtsy and a smile, and Miles walked over and kissed his mother on the cheek. "Hello, Mother. Glad you could come." He hadn't invited her, but then, she never required invitations.

"Oh," she said when she had stepped far enough into the room to see Thomas on the floor. "I thought the baby would surely be gone by now." She looked at Miles with an expression he couldn't identify.

"Yes," he said, crouching down to move one of the garlands from Thomas's reach, "well, we made a trip to the Foundling Hospital, but they wouldn't accept the little lad."

His mother drew back in blinking surprise. "Wouldn't accept him?"

"They are strict in their admissions." He glanced at Lydia and noted how slow and measured her movements were. His mother put her on edge and had for nearly as long as Miles could remember.

"Well"—she took a seat in the nearest chair—"I shouldn't have thought they would be in a position to refuse a donation."

"They don't accept donations, Mother. Not anymore."

She raised her brows. "Perhaps not formally, but everyone accepts the *right* donation. Never mind that, though. What do you intend to do now?"

Miles shrugged and used a foot to sweep some of the greenery bits into a pile. "We will work to find a different situation for him. A family who might take him in after Christmastide."

His mother blinked at him. "I see. Well, I shall endeavor to put the word about myself."

Miles glanced at Lydia, whose eyes had widened. "Thank you, Mother, but we needn't bother you with that. We shall manage, and in the meantime, we are content to have him here."

"Yes, yes," she said, looking to Thomas again. "I cannot deny he is quite charming. I do think that he cannot but add to your stress, though, and I am convinced that if you would both just relax a bit, you might find that you have a child of your own in a very short time. You know, it took nearly half a year before I became pregnant with you, Miles, and I was terribly concerned over it. It wasn't until I took a trip to the countryside and left off thinking of it that I was rewarded."

Miles felt his muscles tensing, and he didn't even dare look at Lydia. It wasn't the first time his mother had suggested that their lack of children was due to something they were doing wrong—or had likened her own experience to theirs, despite the fact that hers was so short-lived in comparison. She was only trying to be helpful, he knew, but such comments couldn't but add to the stress both he and Lydia felt. And their guilt as well. It never failed to make Miles think what his father would say if he were still here and could see just how far Miles was from fulfilling his promise.

It was generally assumed that Lydia was the one to blame for their lack of children, but he found himself questioning the assumption. He'd known more than one situation where the husband of a couple seemingly unable to conceive had died, and his wife had gone on to remarry and have numerous children. It couldn't help but make Miles wonder whether he was the cause of their troubles.

"I do so wish for a grandchild to dote upon," said his mother, settling back into her chair with a sigh. "And to meet the heir of this family. You cannot imagine what pride I felt when you were born, Miles."

"Excuse me," Lydia said, hand to her mouth. "I believe Thomas needs to be fed." She hurriedly picked him up from the floor.

"Can not one of the servants do that?" asked Miles's mother.

"I am more than happy to do it myself," Lydia said, and Miles could hear the slight trembling in her voice. She was gone a moment later, and he debated following after her. Diana and Mary were sharing grimacing glances with one another.

"Thomas, did she say?" Miles's mother asked.

"Yes, that is what we've decided to call him."

She looked thoughtful. "I suppose you must call him something, but I do not think it is wise to become too attached." She looked at the door Lydia had disappeared through. "It really ought to be one of the servants feeding him."

Miles was hardly listening. "Just a moment, Mother. If you'll excuse me." He hurried after his wife, catching sight of her a ways down the corridor.

"Lydia," he said as he came up beside her and slowed.

He heard the sniffing before he saw the tears, which she strove to hide from him, but he placed himself in front of her, stopping her progress, then took her cheek in his hand, wiping at a little rivulet with his thumb. "I am sorry. She doesn't understand."

"But she *thinks* she does." She let Thomas grab the sleeve of her dress and pull it into his mouth.

"Yes." He dropped his hand from her face. "She doesn't mean to hurt, you know."

"Does she not?" Lydia looked at him intently. "Does she not mean to make it clear that you made the wrong decision when you married me?" She looked away. "And you never counter her—you allow her to humiliate me and condescend to me. In front of my sisters."

Miles opened his mouth only to shut it again. He hadn't thought of it that way. "I'm sorry, Lydia. I have become so accustomed to letting Mother say whatever she wishes. She does not brook disagreement very well. It is more unpleasant to contradict her than it is to let her speak and brush aside her words."

"For you, perhaps," Lydia said.

He thought on her words for a moment, wondering how to respond. In the beginning of their marriage, he had so seldom been obliged to think when he was with Lydia. It was all so natural. But now, he analyzed every interaction—before and after it occurred—and he often felt paralyzed with indecision.

"I should go feed Thomas," she said. "I shall only be a quarter of an hour."

He watched with a gathering frown as Lydia disappeared down the corridor.

CHAPTER 8

BRIGHTON 1809

"Look!" Lydia cried as she snatched another shell from the sand before the approaching wave crashed over her feet.

Diana and Mary both came running over, holding their skirts up, gazes on Lydia's hand. "What is it?"

Lydia unfurled her fingers to reveal the pink and white shell. Its peaks and grooves fanned out from the bottom in a pattern that approached perfection more than anything Lydia had ever held.

Diana stretched her hand toward it and rubbed a finger along the creases. "That is beautiful. You seem to have all the luck. I haven't found anything but these small ones." She revealed three mussel shells.

"Those are beautiful, as well," Lydia said. "Look how the colors change in the light."

"Iridescent," Mary said, taking one and turning it from side to side. "That's what it is called when the colors shift at different angles."

Smiling, Lydia watched the rainbow appear with every twist. A muffled yell sounded in the distance, and she glanced over at the group of ladies and gentlemen playing with a cricket ball and bat down the shoreline. They played with no wickets, and they seemed to be getting closer and closer to Lydia and her sisters every time Lydia looked in their direction. Her eyes lingered there for a moment, on the smiling faces whose laughs carried on the breeze, but on one figure in particular—the man she had seen at the lending library yesterday. She could still picture his smile and the kindness in his eyes.

She pulled her gaze away and back to the shell in her hand. "Shall we put these shells with the others?"

Her sisters nodded, and they walked toward the small collection they had set in a small basin in the sand, just out of the tide's reach. A dozen seashells lay there, and they set the new ones carefully on top.

"I think I see some over here," Mary said, and she skipped away, bringing a smile to Lydia's face. She was beginning to act much older now, particularly since they'd come to Brighton, but every now and then, some of her youth would reveal itself as it was now. She was only twelve, after all.

Lydia and Diana followed her, stooping down to inspect what the last wave had brought in. Lydia inspected one, then took it over to set in the pile, taking a moment to spread out the treasures.

The voices of the cricket players crescendoed, and Lydia glanced up in time to see a man running backwards in her direction as a ball arced toward her. She hurried to her feet and stumbled away from it, but not before the man, whose arm reached for the approaching ball, crashed into her, sending them both backward onto the sand.

She rolled away from him and, wincing, put a hand to her side, which had been jabbed by the man's elbow as they'd hit the ground. He turned toward her, his eyes so wide that there was no mistaking their blue hue.

"My greatest apologies, miss," he said in an embarrassed voice. He pushed himself up from the ground and held out his hand to her. In the other hand, he held the cricket ball. Somehow, he had managed to catch it and hold onto it.

Diana and Mary came over as Lydia accepted the man's hand. Not expecting the ease with which he pulled her to her feet, she bumped into him again and hurried to step backward. He wore trousers, a brown waistcoat, and shirtsleeves which were rolled up to his elbows, showcasing muscular forearms, while the ends of his cravat rippled with the breeze.

"Forgive me," she said with an embarrassed smile.

He shook his head in a slow, dazed way, his gaze trained on her with evident curiosity and admiration. "The fault lies entirely with me." His voice was soft and gentle, at odds with his powerful build.

"Are you hurt, Lydia?" Diana asked.

Lydia broke her gaze from the man's, and she shook her head, brushing at her skirts. "No, No. I am well."

He narrowed his eyes at her. "Are you certain? I believe I must have hurt you."

She put a hand to her side, which still throbbed, then shook her head.

"But he has broken all of our seashells!" Mary cried out.

Their heads all turned down, taking in the mess of shattered shells that filled the hollow holding the collection. The pink fan shell Lydia had just found seemed to be intact, though, and she bent to pick it up, only to find that it cracked in four pieces in her hand.

"I am so terribly sorry," he said, reaching for the pieces in Lydia's hand. "I should have looked where I was going. I..." He let out a frustrated breath.

"It is no matter," Lydia said, eyes flitting to the woman who was approaching. She had been at the library, too. "The tide will bring in more shells tomorrow."

He grimaced apologetically, but before he could speak, his arm was taken up by the woman. "Mr. Blakeburn," she said in a breathless voice. "Are you well? I saw you fall and..." Her eyes moved to Lydia and her sisters, and she smiled. She was one of the most beautiful creatures Lydia had ever seen: full lips that stretched in a smile, kind eyes, and ringlets tousled by the breeze framing her face.

"I am perfectly well," Mr. Blakeburn said. "But the same cannot be said for these shells, nor for Miss"—he looked at Lydia questioningly.

"Donnely," she replied. "But I assure you, I am unhurt."

He didn't look away from her, as though he didn't know if he believed her.

"Come, Mr. Blakeburn," said the woman, and she sent a smile at the Donnely sisters while pulling him away.

"Forgive me." He bowed then surrendered to the woman's pull.

Lydia and her sisters watched the departure of the couple for a moment, until Lydia realized that Diana was watching her, not Mr. Blakeburn.

"Mr. Blakeburn and Sophia Kirkland," Diana said. "He is heir to a barony. Rather breathtaking together, aren't they? I believe they are expected to make an announcement soon."

Lydia pulled her eyes away, feeling almost as crushed as the shell in her hands. A ridiculous feeling. "How do you come to know such a thing?" Diana was only seventeen, yet she always knew more about Town gossip than Lydia.

Diana shrugged. "They were at the lending library yesterday, and after they left, the two old women near us were discussing it."

Lydia gathered up the shell remnants, slipping them into her reticule. "I'm sure we can find something to do with these bits and pieces. They are still beautiful."

❅

The Present

Small flakes fluttered to the ground on Christmas morning, and Lydia took Thomas up to the window to show him the marvel of falling snow. He smacked his hand against the window panes as if he might somehow reach through it if he tried hard enough.

"Do you smell that?" she asked him. "Cook must have already begun baking the pastries."

She glanced at the door that connected the bedroom to Miles's, and her brows drew together. Things had felt more strained between them since the incident in the drawing room with his mother. Upon reflection, though, she realized she had not handled things well. She wasn't terribly concerned about how her mother-in-law felt, if indeed she had felt anything upon Lydia's hasty departure. No, it was what she had said to Miles that made her stomach crawl with guilt.

She had been frustrated and hurt by his mother's words, and she had taken it out on him. She *did* want him to stand up to his mother—to tell her not to concern herself with what was not her business. But she wasn't so selfish that she didn't see how it would affect Miles's relationship with his mother if he did.

And, truly, at the heart of it all, what bothered her more than the unsolicited advice from the dowager baroness was the fear she harbored inside, which reared its ugly head every time the woman came for a visit. The dowager and her husband had heavily discouraged Miles from marrying Lydia—the daughter of a physician, be he ever so well-to-do, was not what they had wanted for him—and while the knowledge had affected her relationship with her father- and mother-in-law, it had since begun to affect her relationship with Miles himself.

He had disregarded his parents' counsel, and now he undoubtedly regretted it. How could he not? Had he married Sophia Kirkland, it was a near certainty that he would already have an heir, besides the connections her family had. Miss Kirkland had been an eminently eligible choice, and no matter how hard she tried, Lydia had never been able to find fault with the woman.

But none of that justified Lydia's unkindness to Miles. Quite the reverse, rather.

"Shall we go see if Miles is awake?" With her heart pattering against her chest, she took Thomas over to the door and knocked gently upon it.

She heard some muted sounds coming from the other side, and it was a moment before the door opened, revealing Miles with his dressing gown askew and eyes clearly still accustoming themselves to the light.

"Is everything all right?" he asked with concern, rubbing at one of his eyes with a finger.

"Oh, yes, yes, of course," Lydia said, taking a step back. "I am so sorry. I didn't mean to wake you. It must be earlier than I had thought."

Was this what it had come to? A visit from his wife signified something ominous?

He smiled a bit blearily. "Don't apologize." He chucked Thomas gently under the chin. "You are a wonderful sight to wake to. I think I must have overslept. I didn't sleep terribly well last night."

"Nor did I," she said, searching his face. Had he stayed awake for the same reason she had? "Thomas and I wanted to wish you a Merry Christmas." She gathered her courage. "And I wished to apologize for my behavior yesterday."

He blinked twice then shook his head. "No, it is I who owe you an apology."

She smiled, and he followed suit.

"And what of you, Thomas?" Miles asked. "Have you no apology? For all your attempts to ingest our decorations yesterday? Hmm?"

Lydia laughed. Thomas had not only surprised them by turning over and beginning to attempt a crawl, they had also been obliged to pull a handful of greenery from his mouth. "It appears no apology is forthcoming. He seems quite remorseless."

Miles squinted at Thomas. "Ingrate! Shall we go down to breakfast?"

Lydia nodded.

Miles stepped back and hesitated, hand on the door. He held her gaze then dropped his to his dressing gown, still untied.

Lydia's eyes followed, taking in the view of his unbuttoned shirt-sleeves which revealed a great deal of his chest. Had he always been so athletic? Yes, she rather thought he had. She could almost remember how it felt to lay her hand there.

"I just need to change..."

"Oh," Lydia said, blinking away her thoughts. "Of course. I do as well. And Thomas needs to be changed." She kept her eyes safely fixed on his face, but even the line of his jaw led to his neck, which led down—

"Was there something else?" he asked.

"No," she laughed away her thoughts. "Perhaps we can meet in the corridor in a few minutes?"

"Gladly," he said, and she stepped out of the doorway before her eyes could wander again.

She focused on pulling the bell and deciding what she would wear for the day, paying no attention to the quicker-than-usual beating of her heart. It had been a very long time since she had felt the inklings of desire. Intimacy had come to feel like a burden—one that Miles had never seemed to mind in the least. She had forgotten what it was like to hold her husband and be held by him without an eye toward whether things might result in what they had been hoping for for so long.

Ten minutes later, they joined one another in the corridor and made their way downstairs.

The dining room had been chosen after the drawing room and staircase for decoration, and it presented a very cozy picture indeed: fire crackling in the grate, juniper branches draped atop the mantel, and a collection of holly set in the middle of the table.

To Lydia's surprise, Diana and Mary soon joined them for breakfast.

"I didn't wish to sleep away the entire day," Diana said as she sat down. "It is Christmas, after all. And I thought we would need to be on our way to church soon."

"You are correct," said Miles. "It is normally a short journey to church—a few minutes in the carriage—but with the snow and the ice, it will be best if we leave a bit earlier than usual. We will need to get Thomas set with the servants as well." He glanced at the baby, who was reaching for Lydia's cup of tea.

"Oh," she said, pushing the tea out of reach.

Miles looked at her searchingly. "What?"

She tore a small piece from her toast and gave it to Thomas. "I... it's nothing." She hadn't considered the fact that Thomas wouldn't be accompanying them to church.

"We cannot possibly take him with us," Miles said.

"Can we not?" Lydia asked.

"If the service is anything like ours at home," Mary chimed in, "I wouldn't mind a bit of distraction while the vicar drones on and on."

Miles didn't seem to hear Mary's comment. His eyes were trained on Lydia, and she felt them boring into her, while his wrists rested on the table as though he intended to solve things before applying himself to his food again.

"My dear," he said, "I don't particularly wish to spend Christmas explaining to people how we come to suddenly have a six-month-old child."

"Surely it is none of their business," Lydia said.

"No, certainly not," he said. "But when did that ever stop anyone? I can't imagine you wish to explain it any more than I do. It will draw attention to something we have taken pains to avoid drawing attention to."

Thomas was playing with her fingers, and she watched his movements rather than meeting Miles's gaze. She *didn't* want to answer all the questions that taking Thomas with them would elicit. They could explain that they had taken in a foundling for a short time, but the questions and assumptions would hardly stop there, and Lydia had no desire to receive the pity and the suggestions that would follow. Those interactions were as tiresome as they were disheartening.

She might have borne the assumptions people made about her and Miles if only people had kept them to themselves. Instead, they insisted on conveying their opinions directly to her. Miles had to bear with but a fraction of the conversations Lydia did, as it was assumed she was the one at fault. Even the vicar had implied in a few of his comments to her that greater dedication to God might garner happy results.

But, even more than all of that, she was bothered by a suspicion that Miles's reluctance to take Thomas was rooted in his concern about how it would make him appear—taking in the child of another man because his wife couldn't provide him with their own. Undoubtedly, he didn't want to give people the reminder of his and Lydia's failure.

"I suppose you are right," she said with a swallow. "I shall call for Jane."

It took time for her to convey the instructions to the maid, and when she finally finished and handed Thomas off to her, it was to turn toward an amused Diana.

"What?" Lydia said, trying not to betray how difficult she found it to leave Thomas with someone else.

"You've entirely overwhelmed the poor girl," Diana responded, linking her arm with Lydia's. "It will be a miracle if she remembers the half of what you said. But that cannot matter too greatly, as we are not leaving on a month-long holiday, my love. We are only going to church for a bit."

The snow was coming down more quickly than before, and Miles had been wise to call for the carriage early. Not only were they obliged to stop for the dowager baroness first, the driver had to adopt an inching pace to avoid the horses and the carriage slipping on the pockets of ice that covered their route to the church.

The church building itself was cold on the inside, and no one shed their coats as the group of them made their way to the box pew. Lydia made sure to introduce her sisters to people she thought might interest them. Diana and Mary were both engaging in manners and pleasing in appearance, and people seemed eager to meet them, so it was not until the vicar was ready to begin the service that they finally slipped into the pew.

Lydia's attention wandered for a time, only to be pulled back by the words of the vicar.

"Who would take in Joseph, Mary, and the Christ child? No one. The very Messiah—the Savior of the world—was left to be born in the most lowly of circumstances. Born in a manger and wrapped in swaddling clothes. And are we not guilty of just such abandonment? Of shutting our hearts and homes to Christ? Of choosing sin and entertainment over He alone who is mighty to save?"

Lydia's thoughts turned to Thomas, found, just like the Christ child, in a manger, wrapped in nothing but blankets. He had already been a blessing to her. She might never bear a child, but if nothing else, she would care for this one while he needed her. She would not neglect her Christian duty, and she hoped God would bless her for it.

Thomas was asleep when they arrived back at the townhouse, and Lydia smiled down at him in the cradle, grateful for the opportunity to care for such an innocent soul, even if it was only temporarily.

He slept long—all through the time Lydia and her sisters spent helping to package the treats and food in brown paper, tied with string, and he was still not awake by the time they left to deliver everything to the Foundling Hospital. A wagon was loaded with the prepared food, covered, and driven behind the coach.

Upon their arrival, Mr. Moss greeted and showed them into the same building Lydia and Miles had stood in. He expressed gratitude on behalf of the hospital and the children for their kindness. "It is not every day they are given such a treat. I shall just call for some of the staff to unload the wagon."

"Oh," Diana said, bringing him up short. "Is there any way we might deliver the gifts to them ourselves? There are three great baskets of bread you might give them at dinner, but we wrapped some treats individually and wondered if we might hand each child one."

Lydia stifled the desire to embrace her sister. Diana could be shockingly forward sometimes, but that wasn't always a bad thing.

Mr. Moss hesitated then glanced at his pocketwatch. "I suppose so. They are just about to finish the church service, and the children will have the next hour free. Let me go speak with the instructors. I shall return in a moment."

When he did, it was with happy news. "Perhaps you will regret your request when I tell you this," Mr. Moss said, "but I think the best way to go about it will be to have you distribute the gifts in the courtyard. It is quite cold, and I shall understand if you change your minds, but given that the wagon is there and that the courtyard has the greatest amount of space required for the type of queue we will have..." He looked a question at them.

Lydia glanced at Miles, intending to ask him what he thought of such an idea. But she might have spared herself.

"Oh, I am sure we do not regard the cold," Diana said with a dismissive wave of the hand.

And so it was decided. Within a few minutes, the queue of children was forming, each of them wearing a brown dress or short coat beneath a coat more suitable for winter.

Situated right next to the wagon, Lydia and the others took the individually packaged treats and greeted each child. Some met them with grateful smiles and wide, curious eyes, which lingered on the package being offered. A few even wrapped their arms around Lydia, only to be chastised by their instructors. But it was the faces which were serious or even wary that tugged on Lydia's heart the most.

She glanced at Miles as he greeted a little girl. She was small enough that she must have returned to the hospital recently from her years in the country, and the fear in her eyes touched Lydia's heart. But Miles was quickly able to elicit a smile and a laugh from the girl, and Lydia felt a gush of appreciation for her husband.

She turned back to address the child in front of her, a boy of about eight or nine years with dark hair and thick brows which frowned heavily.

"Merry Christmas, my dear," she said, extending the brown paper package toward him. He refused to meet her gaze, and she reached for his hand, turning it palm up to receive the gift. Her heart stopped at the sight of the lash marks there.

He lowered his eyes, and she reached for his other hand. It was free of marks, and she put the gift in it, forcing down the emotion in her throat.

"That present is just for you," she said. "I hope you shall like it."

His eyes flicked toward her, but as their gazes met, he hurriedly turned his away.

"What is your name?" she asked.

He didn't look at her, and she barely caught what he said. "Matthew."

Matthew. She pressed her lips together, swallowing down her emotion. "God bless you, Matthew. You are precious to Him. Merry Christmas."

He met her gaze for a moment then turned away without a word.

"What sweet children," Mary said in a misty voice as they settled into the carriage a short time later, rubbing their hands together to warm them. She looked through the window where the end of the queue of children disappeared into one of the buildings.

Diana put a hand to her own cheek. "One of the boys kissed me to say thank you."

Lydia was still trying to rein in her emotions, and she felt Miles's hand close around hers. She looked up at him, and he sent her a sad smile. He understood.

Diana seemed to notice her sister's somberness too. "What is it, Lydia?"

Lydia managed a smile and shook her head. "Nothing. I just...I couldn't help thinking of what the vicar said today each time I looked into the faces of those children. Christ deserved much better than life gave Him, and so do those children."

Miles squeezed her hand tighter. "Well, they are happier now than they were before we came, surely."

She nodded. "But it is such a little thing we did. I wish it was more. I wish each one of them had a home."

"And you would give it to them if you could," Miles said. "But the hospital is much better than what most of them would face if it didn't exist. They are more fortunate than others."

He was right, but it was little consolation to her.

She tried to shake off her melancholy, and the view of Thomas accomplished just that, for his mouth stretched into a smile at the sight of her. She took him from Jane and embraced him tightly, setting a kiss upon his head. "Merry Christmas, Thomas," she said softly.

The dowager baroness joined them for Christmas Dinner, and Lydia was grateful that she refrained from commenting when her gaze fell upon Thomas. She seemed determined to be pleasant, and Lydia was too.

Dish after dish was brought to the table in a seeming never-ending array of culinary delights, among which were mincemeat pies, roast duck, and a creamy white soup.

"Well," said the dowager as she was served mincemeat pie, "I must say, your cook has truly outdone herself today."

"She has," Lydia said. "Particularly considering how last night we sprang upon her all the bread and tarts we wished her to bake for the foundlings. She certainly deserves a large bonus." She looked to Miles, and he nodded.

"I do need to arrange all of that," he said.

There was a brief pause.

"Miles, my dear," said his mother. "I imagine you saw the Hardales at church today. I spoke with Lady Hardale, and she was pleased to convey the news to me that Sophia is with child again—their third, as I'm sure you know."

Lydia's hand clenched her fork, knuckles white, body stiff. She felt her husband's gaze on her, and she focused on cutting the roast duck on her plate.

"That is happy news indeed," Miles said, taking a sip from his wine glass.

"Yes," replied his mother. "Not so long ago, I saw their first child

—a boy you know—and he is such a taking little thing. He looks set already to step into his father's shoes as Baron Venton. In any case, I took the liberty of sending your congratulations."

"Thank you, Mother," said Miles.

Lydia finally looked up, too desperate to see Miles's reaction to keep her head down any longer. He was looking down at his plate, and his quiet demeanor and the somber expression on his face cut Lydia deeper than she was prepared for.

She could see it in his face. He regretted his decision to marry her. It might have been Sophia Kirkland sitting here now, with a baby growing in her belly and one already asleep for the night.

Instead, Miles was housing a foundling and married to a barren wife.

CHAPTER 9

BRIGHTON 1809

Miles conveyed Miss Kirkland to her mother, who smiled benevolently upon him.

"With more of your instruction," said Lady Hardale, "Sophia will be quite a proficient cricket player, Lord Lynham."

He glanced down the coastline, where the three young women were making their way up the beach toward the town. He turned back toward Lady Hardale, trying to stifle his restlessness. "I cannot claim any credit, being only passable at the sport myself."

"You are too modest," said Miss Kirkland. "We all saw how you managed to catch that ball. And, Mother, you are too generous. I think I shall never be proficient, but I do enjoy it."

"Why do you not join us for dinner, Lord Lynham," asked Lady Hardale. "It would be our pleasure to host you."

He grimaced in apology. "I wish I could, but I'm afraid I have a matter requiring my attention just now."

"Tomorrow, then," she replied.

He bowed in acceptance. "I would be delighted."

Lady Hardale and her daughter took their leave, and he watched them go, waving a hand at Miss Kirkland when, where the sand ended, she turned to look at him. He tipped his head to the side as he waited for them to disappear. She was lovely. Nothing at all about her to give him hesitation—nor reason to spend the last fifteen minutes wondering about the young woman he'd toppled over and whose seashell collection he'd obliterated. There was a sweetness in Miss Donnelly's face and demeanor that had made Miles reluctant to leave her. He was confident that she had been more hurt than she'd let on.

Once Sophia and her mother disappeared from sight, he turned away, looking for the three young women. But there was no sign of them. He hit his hand against his leg in disappointment and turned back toward the waves.

But early in the afternoon the next day as he sat on the beach, he sighted the sisters again, coming over the crest of the sandy hill that led down toward the water. He felt the pace of his heart increase and wondered if perhaps he was being overly forward. But he wanted to make things right—and he couldn't resist his curiosity—so he rose from his seated position and made his way over to them.

He came upon Miss Donnely first. She held a basket on her arm.

"I see you've taken precautionary measures," he said.

She looked up at him and blinked quickly in surprise then glanced down at the basket and smiled. "It was silly of us to set them upon the ground, but it was an impromptu activity. We had only come for a walk." She glanced behind her, where one of her sisters bent down, though it was clear her gaze was trained upon Miles and Lydia.

"I hoped I might find you here today," he said. "I couldn't help feeling that you weren't being fully honest yesterday about not being injured. I can't imagine that being hurtled into by fifteen stone could leave a person none the worse."

She laughed softly, a beautiful, melodious sound that made him smile all the wider.

"It only hurt for a bit," she said with a shrug. "You needn't worry yourself."

He twisted his mouth to the side, but he didn't want to press her, so he held out his hand. "I bring an offering. I know it is but small, and certainly no replacement for what you had collected yesterday, but"—*his heart hammered*—"I thought it might interest you if you like seashells."

Mouth open in surprise, she looked at his hand then up at his eyes. "But...but," *she said.*

He nodded at her to take it. "It is yours. Consider it an apology."

It was a beautiful specimen: white and caramel colored, and shaped like a tulip before blooming. He had spent nigh on an hour combing the beach for shells after Lady Hardale and Miss Kirkland's departure yesterday, and when he had happened upon this one, all his efforts had felt rewarded.

And they were doubly rewarded now with the look of awe in Miss Donnely's eyes as she picked up the shell, twisting it and turning it in her hands, then smiling at him as though he'd offered her a pearl. "I've never seen anything like it," *she said.*

"Nor I," *he responded.*

"Where did you find it?" *she asked.* "Here? On this same beach?"

"I can show you, if you'd like," *he said.*

A hint of caution entered her eyes, and she hesitated.

"All of you," *he said, nodding at her sisters.*

She smiled. "We should like that very much."

❋

The Present

Miles rummaged through the papers in the folio on his study desk in search of the one that detailed the wages for the servants at the townhouse. It was St. Stephen's Day, and he had told the servants to present themselves in the kitchen at nine before most of them took the rest of the day off. The ones who remained would have tomorrow off.

He found the correct paper and ran his finger down the column name by name, stopping with each one to calculate and then take the correct amount of coins out of his purse. At Lynham Place, his steward would be doing the same thing, he hoped. He wanted the servants to know they were appreciated, and some extra coins in their pocket would hopefully convey that message, as well as giving them a merry start to a day they could spend with family or friends.

As for him, Lydia, and his sisters-in-law, they had agreed that they would spend the day relaxing in the house and making do with the bread, cold meats, and soup that Cook had spent the past few days preparing. After their time in the cold at the Foundling Hospital the day before, no one seemed eager to leave the warmth of the house.

Diana and Mary would, as usual, be staying abed late, so once Miles had finished distributing the servant bonuses and bid the last of them good day, he lingered in the kitchen for a moment, looking at the array of food available for breakfast. An idea occurred to him, and he took one of the stacked silver trays on the table and set about filling it with food items he thought might appeal to Lydia and Thomas. It was an idea he would have brushed off if it weren't for Thomas's presence in the household. He gave Miles courage he might not otherwise have had—and an excuse to see his wife.

A few minutes later, he made his way up the kitchen stairs, down the corridor, then up the second set of stairs, a little smile hovering on his lips at the picture he presented, tray in hand. When he came to Lydia's room, he ran a quick hand through his hair and tapped lightly upon the door, stifling the urge to fidget as he waited. He could just barely hear the sounds of Thomas's cooing.

The door opened slightly, and Lydia appeared in the gap, the frown on her face transforming to surprise.

"Miles," she said. "I couldn't imagine whom it might be, for I thought you gave the servants the day off." She was wearing only a shift, and she wrapped an arm over her body as if to hide it, rubbing the other arm as if she was cold. Her eyes went to the tray in Miles's hands, and she looked back up at him. "What is this?"

"Breakfast? I thought you and Thomas might be hungry."

She looked back over her shoulder, where Thomas was lying on a blanket on the floor, holding his toes with his hands and babbling, a sound which seemed to be increasing in volume. She laughed. "Yes, I think he especially is." She opened the door wider, and Miles gave her a thankful smile as he stepped in.

He walked over to where Thomas lay and hesitated for a moment, while Lydia went to her armoire and pulled out a wrapper, slinging her arms through the sleeves and tying it in place. Miles didn't miss the hurriedness of the gesture, as if she was afraid of what he might see. As though he hadn't seen it all before.

He set the tray on the floor, and Lydia gave him a funny look.

He shrugged. "I am embracing the casual nature of this breakfast."

She laughed and followed him down to the floor so that they were on either side of Thomas. Lydia tucked her legs beneath her and leaned on a hand, smiling down at the baby.

"All right," she said to him. "Yes, we hear you."

Miles reached for one of the loaves of bread left over from Cook's preparations for the Foundling Hospital and tore off a tiny piece, offering it to Thomas. The baby's eyes widened as they focused in on the bread, and the noise stopped, his attention too much taken up by the task of reaching for what Miles was extending toward him.

"Here," Lydia said, pulling Thomas up to a sitting position.

"Can he sit by himself?" Miles allowed Thomas to take the small piece of bread and put it in his mouth.

"I don't know," Lydia said.

"Why not let him try?"

"What if he falls?"

"He won't. We shall catch him." He scooted closer. "We can both put a hand behind him."

Lydia nodded, but she looked a bit nervous. Miles set a hand just behind Thomas's body, which bounced up and down as he reveled in the food he had been given.

Miles gave a nod, and Lydia slowly pulled her hand away from the baby's back. There was a moment of apprehension and a slight rocking backwards by Thomas which brought his feet off the floor, but he managed to right himself.

"He did it!" Lydia said. "You're sitting all by yourself, Thomas. Look at you! Look at him, Miles!"

Thomas turned his head toward her, wobbling slightly as he redistributed his weight.

"What a clever boy you are," she said, and Miles found that his own eyes insisted upon flitting back to Lydia again and again. She wasn't nearly as guarded when she was around Thomas, and watching her smile and behave without any affectation was like stepping back into the past—a past he ached to return to.

Thomas seemed to be enjoying his newfound independence, and his eyes roved about the room, finally landing upon the food on the tray before him. Miles laughed at the way his eyes widened at the sight.

"Precisely how I feel about food," Miles said.

Thomas leaned forward, and, just in time, Miles reached out a hand to prevent him from falling forward onto the silver tray.

"Oh my!" Lydia said, coming to Thomas's aid as well, as his nose hovered just inches above a plate of ham. Together, they pulled him back to a sitting position,.

"Well," Miles said, "if either of us are to have a moment's peace, I had better hold this little chap"—he picked him up and set him in his lap—"so we can eat." He pulled Thomas's hand away from the tray. "Yes, yes, I will share with you. Not as though I shall have any choice in the matter."

The three of them shared breakfast together, and there were smiles on all their faces as they watched the baby's antics, and his reactions to the bits of food they felt they could offer him.

"He doesn't seem to be terribly fond of that marmalade, does he?" Lydia said, wiping some of it from Thomas's lips with a napkin.

"No, he does not. Don't worry, Thomas. We shan't tell Cook, for she is quite proud of it. A family recipe, I believe."

Never had Miles lingered so long at breakfast, but he would have gladly remained there through the morning, laughing and talking with Lydia, taking turns holding Thomas, if there had not finally come a knock on the door.

Lydia frowned. "Who could that be?" She handed Thomas back to Miles and rose to her feet, hurrying to the door in a graceful but quick-toed maneuver—she had always been light on her feet.

"Here you are!" Diana said, trying to look beyond Lydia into the room. "I knocked on the door of the other room, but there was no answer, and then I thought I heard voices in here. We thought to find you in the dining room for breakfast."

"Oh, well, Miles brought up a tray from the kitchen, so we decided to take it in here with Thomas instead."

Diana's head peeked into the room, and she smiled widely as her eyes landed upon Thomas. "Good morning, little ray of sunshine."

Mary's head appeared next, and she smiled too. "What a cozy breakfast you are having."

Miles smiled, but if Diana and Mary believed that this was representative of his and Lydia's life, they could hardly be more mistaken. He only hoped Diana wouldn't ask her any more questions about why they were in this bedchamber rather than Miles's.

"If you'd like some of the food, I'm sure Miles and Thomas wouldn't mind," Lydia said.

"I wouldn't," Miles said. "But I cannot speak for this fellow. He will gladly offer you the marmalade, but I think he might consume all the bread and butter himself if given the opportunity."

"Oh, I am not hungry," Diana said with a wave of the hand. "I only wished to ask Miles if he might consider inviting his brother—and his friends, perhaps—to join us for games later today?"

Miles set Thomas on his back on the rug and rose from the floor.

"I could, I suppose. If he doesn't already have plans, that is, which, knowing Harry, I admit I should be surprised to discover."

Diana shrugged. "Well, it can't harm to ask, can it?"

"I shall send a note and see what I can discover."

Diana gave a satisfied smile. "Thank you, Miles. You are the greatest of brothers-in-law."

"Not to mention the only one," he said wryly, but Diana and Mary were both already chatting about what games would do best for a group of three or four men and three women as they shut the door behind them.

Lydia gave a great sigh and turned back toward Miles and Thomas. "I fear that the two of them are turning into silly girls. Oh, Miles," Lydia said, covering a laugh with her hand while her eyes were trained on his face.

"What?"

She picked up a napkin from the tray and took a step toward him. "Either you are a very messy eater, or Thomas must have flung some of the marmalade onto your chin when he was trying to rid himself of it." She reached it to his face, rubbing gently at a spot on the right side of his chin.

He submitted to her ministrations with a quickened heartbeat, staring at the way her brow furrowed ever-so-slightly in concentration. He never had the opportunity to study her face anymore. He thought he had memorized it, an indelible engraving in his mind after all the hours he'd stared at her. But as he studied her now, he realized he had forgotten many of the little details.

"That is some very sticky marmalade," she said with a final wipe. She looked up at him and narrowed her eyes. "What? What are you smiling at?"

His brows drew together. "Was I smiling?"

She nodded.

"Then I was smiling at you," he said, and his own daring frightened him.

Immediately, a shyness took over her, and she tucked a stray lock of hair behind her ear with an uneasy chuckle. "Am I so amusing?"

He shook his head. *You are adorable and beautiful.* It's what he would have said if he hadn't seen the wariness creep into her eyes while he was looking at her. "You are simply very thorough."

"Well, perhaps I shouldn't have said anything. Should I, Thomas?" She picked up the baby. "Then Miles could have gone all day with dried marmalade on his face."

"That reminds me," Miles said, "I need to send a message to Harry, though he is undoubtedly still abed. I hope your sisters are not expecting too much of him and his friends. They are likely to be disappointed. My brother could certainly compete with your sisters for silliness."

To Miles's great surprise, a response from Harry arrived within an hour of his note being sent over, and he felt the eyes of Lydia's sisters watch him intently as the servant delivered it to him in the morning room.

The women were engaged in making decorations out of colored paper. At first, Thomas had been mesmerized by the mere sight of the paper, but now he seemed intent on participating in the folding—and consumption—of the paper. Despite the distraction he was, Lydia maintained that she preferred to hold him.

"I want him to experience it all," she had said as she pulled his hand away from his mouth a second too late.

"Well, he certainly is doing just that," Miles had responded with a quivering smile as he opened Harry's letter.

His eyes ran over it quickly, and his mouth quirked up as he reached the end. He looked up and paused, eyes moving between Diana's, Mary's, and Lydia's faces, all staring at him. Only the baby seemed disinterested, taking advantage of the lack of supervisions to slam his hand on the table, as if in demand that the paper be moved closer to him again.

"What, Thomas?" Miles said. "Have you no desire to know whether or not Harry intends to come for games?"

"Well?" Diana said impatiently. "What did he say?"

Miles said nothing for a moment. He was enjoying the power he held over the Donnely sisters too much to relinquish it right away. But, even more than that, he wanted to see whether he could make Lydia smile. "He...said...." Miles said the words with exaggerated deliberation.

Diana prompted him with her head and eyes, and Lydia's efforts to stifle her amusement were less and less successful by the second.

Miles pretended to notice a spot on his sleeve and focused his efforts on removing it. He looked up and found Lydia watching him with an expression of half-enjoyment, half-censure. It was enough to satisfy him, and his mouth drew into a wide grin. "My apologies. What was I saying? Ah yes, he said he and Robinson will come at five. So we may expect him close to six, I'd wager."

Both Diana and Mary let out relieved sighs. "You are an unbearable tease, Miles," Diana said, and she took Mary by the hand. "Now we must settle on what games to play."

CHAPTER 10

CHRISTMAS EVE 1809

Lydia watched with a smile as Miles looked around at the boughs of greenery that hung above each doorway, her hand held within his.

"You are certainly more festive than we have ever been at Lynham Place," he said. "I am beginning to feel as though I have been deprived my whole life. It is amazing how such a little thing can change the entire atmosphere of a place."

She cocked her head to the side, admiring the nearest bough. "It does make things feel more cheery, doesn't it?"

"Certainly. I hope your parents won't be offended if I follow their lead in the future at Lynham Place."

She shook her head. "We are meant to start our own traditions now that we are to become a family, are we not? But you haven't even seen the best part of the decorations yet." She shot him an enigmatic look and led him to the next doorway, where a kissing bough hung.

He raised a brow at her. "Is that what I think it is?"

She only smiled as he glanced furtively up and down the corridor *then pulled her into his arms. "I understand we are meant to take a berry for every kiss," he said.*

Lydia shrugged, chills running up her arms and down her neck as his face grew nearer. "So they say. I have never availed myself of the bough before."

Miles reached up and plucked a berry from the bough. Then another. And another. And another.

"Miles!" Lydia said in a scandalized whisper.

"What?" he continued pulling berries until she grasped his hands and held them down. He laughed and leaned in toward her, close enough that they would have been kissing had both of their lips not been pulled into laughing smiles. Their noses touched, though, and he nuzzled his against hers. "I am merely planning ahead. I assure you, these will all be used."

Berries gripped in his hand, he wrapped his arms around her waist and closed the remaining distance between them, locking their lips together.

※

The Present

By a quarter after six, Diana was tapping a foot on the ground, unable to hide her impatience at the tardiness of their visitors. Mary sat on the sofa, holding Thomas so that he stood on her legs, something which delighted him greatly, and Lydia too, as a spectator.

Approaching footsteps and muted voices sounded outside the room, and the door opened. Under the kissing bough Diana and Mary had together created—and its berries still untouched—Harry stepped into the room, followed by Robinson. Harry was a handsome young man of twenty-six, with little thought of marriage and every thought of enjoying the many entertainments available to him as a bachelor. He was narrower of face than his elder brother and freer with his smiles.

Miles had been right when he had said that Harry was accounted the more handsome of the two, but Lydia had never subscribed to such a belief. She liked Harry and enjoyed his company on the infrequent occasions when it was offered, but he was like an exaggerated version of Miles. She liked short and infrequent doses of Harry, where she could spend hours with Miles and never tire of his company.

Or she used to be able to, at least. It had been some time since they had spent such a substantial amount of time together.

Harry gallantly kissed Lydia's hand, earning him an impatient rolling of the eyes from Miles, who performed the introductions between Harry and his friend and Lydia's sisters. Lydia didn't miss the admiration for both gentlemen in Diana's and Mary's eyes, and she was glad for it. They needed some excitement, and Harry and his friend were just the people to provide it. She certainly didn't begrudge them a bit of flirtation. They were both intelligent enough to know it for what it was.

Harry was naturally full of questions about Thomas, but he seemed to take the responses Miles provided without batting an eye.

Miles invited Diana and Mary to take charge and inform the group of what delights were in store, and Harry and Robinson took seats, the former stretching out his legs in front of him with his ankles crossed, very much at home. Miles came to sit beside Lydia, offering to take Thomas for a time, which she allowed him to do. She liked watching Miles care for Thomas nearly as much as she liked holding Thomas herself.

Diana and Mary stood in front of everyone, looking for all the world as though they were about to commence a grand affair in front of thousands.

"Tonight's entertainment," said Diana with a smile that promised an irregular treat, "will begin with a game of Musical Magic."

Lydia and the other three looked at one another, each of them evidently as confused as the others.

Diana watched them, awaiting a proper reaction, then frowned. "Have you never played Musical Magic?"

The four of them shook their heads, and Diana and Mary shared a look of eager anticipation. Mary gave her sister a nod.

"One person will be sent out of the room," Diana explained. "Those of us remaining will decide upon an object in the room and a task that must be performed with that object. When the absent person returns, it is his or her job to determine which object and what task we have selected. Mary here"—she put out a hand to display her sister—"will be at the piano, playing a tune that will get louder as the person strays away from the object and softer as he or she approaches it. Once the correct object is discovered, the music will recommence—loud if he or she is incorrect in discovering what task must be performed with the object, soft as the task is detected. Are there any questions?"

Robinson raised his hand immediately. "Who goes first?"

Diana smiled widely. "You. Thank you for volunteering."

He threw his head back with a laugh but rose to his feet. "Very well. I shall just go out of the room, then? And you will retrieve me in the corridor when you have hit upon the object and task?"

Diana gave a nod, and Robinson left the room. Guided by Diana and Harry—who seemed to be reaching a quick understanding—it was a matter of just two minutes before the rest of them had decided upon just what object and task Robinson should be assigned, Thomas being the object and a waltz the task.

Lydia held Thomas on her lap. He was blissfully unaware of what lay in store for him, content to focus on the tassels of the nearest pillow. His eyes bulged, though, at the sound of the loud chord played by Mary when Robinson first entered the room, signaling that he was nowhere near the object. Robinson hurried into the room, and the music grew a bit softer. He was quick to discover that the music was faintest as he neared the sofa Lydia sat upon, but it took some trial and error—including picking up the pillow Thomas was holding, resulting in angry squawking until the tassels were back in reach.

Finally, Robinson tilted his head to the side and looked at Thomas himself.

Lydia, Miles, Diana, and Harry all laughed at the look of uncertainty on Robinson's face. He put out his hands toward Thomas, and Mary tapped as gently as she could on the keys, stopping them completely when Robinson took Thomas in his arms.

"What task am I to do with a baby?" Robinson asked.

"That," Diana said, "you are strictly prohibited from asking. I am sure you will solve it in no time at all."

That he was meant to dance with Thomas, he did indeed discover in less than a minute. But precisely which dance was a matter that required more guesswork, and by the time he had tried the steps to a cotillion, a scotch reel, and the boulanger, the three people on the sofa were in stitches from laughing, and Mary's piano playing had taken a serious turn for the worse due to her own difficulty in keeping her composure. Thomas, on the other hand, was torn between laughs and hilarious looks of uncertainty as Robinson tried to guide him through the arm movements required of him.

It was only when he finally gave Thomas back to Lydia that she realized that, in her mirth, she had set a steadying hand upon Miles's leg, and he had a hand on her back. She slowly removed hers, though she felt reluctant to do so.

"I think I will have to cry off the second dance in our set, chap," Robinson said in a slightly breathless voice as he tousled Thomas's hair and turned toward Harry. "I nominate you to be the next *victim*."

Harry looked to Diana, who gave a consenting nod.

He pushed himself to a stand, brushing off his coat sleeves with a wide grin at his friend. "It took you a full seven minutes to grasp what we were asking of you, Robinson. I wager I shall do so in half the time."

Robinson snorted as he settled into the chair Harry had been in. "We shall see, Blakeburn!" he shouted as the door closed behind Harry.

This time, it was Robinson who guided the choice of object and task, and it was quite clear he meant to have his revenge upon Harry. He wore a satisfied smirk as he let Harry back into the room.

Lydia rocked Thomas gently in her arms while keeping an eye on Diana. Either she wasn't nervous, or she was very good at masking it.

Robinson tapped the face on the pocketwatch in his hand. "Time is ticking."

Music emanated in deafening chords as Harry made his way quickly around the outer rim of the drawing room. Seeing his choice was ineffective, he came to the center of the room, bringing about a quick softening of the music. He shot Robinson a victorious look then went to the candlestick which sat upon the small table beside the sofa. The music grew louder, so he went back the other way, passing Miles then Lydia as the volume eased only to crescendo once he passed by Diana. He stopped in his tracks and took two steps backward. The music went soft, and he turned toward Diana on the couch, a curious half-smile on his face.

Only someone as familiar with Diana as Lydia was would have noticed the slight pink in her cheeks—which only enhanced her natural beauty—or the way she held her hands a bit too primly in her lap. She *was* nervous.

Harry put out a hand in invitation for her to stand, and the music grew louder. He frowned then turned around to take the seat next to her, which required Lydia to scoot closer to Miles, who was at the far end of the sofa and couldn't move. Her thigh bumped into Miles's hand, and he pulled it from between them, hesitating for a moment before setting his arm on the back of the sofa behind her where it rested lightly on her shoulders. Thomas was nearly asleep, and Lydia's right arm was beginning to tire, so she let it rest on Miles's leg. Miles smiled at her and caressed Thomas's head with a gentle thumb.

Before Harry could sit next to Lydia, though, the piano music grew louder again, and he was obliged to leave off the idea, instead coming to stand before her yet again. Lydia debated whether she should move into the space again available to her, but it was too comfortable with the warmth of Miles's arm on her shoulders and his leg supporting her arm. Thomas's head was heavy.

Robinson had his pocket watch out by now and was tapping the glass on it teasingly.

Harry screwed up his face in thought then, with a suspicious narrowing of the eyes, looked at his friend. Robinson grinned, as though to confirm whatever Harry had suspected.

Gaze still fixed on Robinson, Harry began bending his knees, and the volume of chords at the piano weakened slightly. Harry laughed and lowered all the way down to a knee. Diana was looking at him expectantly, as if she hadn't the slightest idea why he was kneeling before her. Harry looked to the others for any sign of what he was meant to do, but the only response he received was laughs. Lydia tried her best to stifle hers so as not to disturb Thomas, who seemed to be settling in for a much-needed slumber.

Harry reached tentatively for Diana's hand and was rewarded with a further softening of the music. He inclined his head as if he finally understood what was expected of him and twisted off the single ring he wore.

"It would do me the greatest honor, Miss Donnely," said Harry as the music finally stopped, "if you would consent to be my wife." He put the ring onto one of Diana's fingers and set a kiss upon the back of her hand in a gesture so charming, Lydia thought it might be a miracle if Diana's heart was untouched by it.

Diana feigned surprise and fluttered her lashes in faux coquetry. "I am terribly flattered, Mr. Blakeburn, except the ring you've given me was evidently fitted for another woman's hand."

Lydia laughed along with the rest of them, but she felt a little aching in her heart at the flirtation between Diana and Harry. She and Miles had used to be just so. It seemed an age, and Lydia missed it terribly all of a sudden, the sight bringing her heart into her throat. She glanced at Miles beside her, and she didn't miss the look of wistfulness—or the hint of sadness—in the smile he wore.

Harry and Diana continued their bantering flirtation, and Lydia attempted to rise from the sofa. Miles gave her a questioning look and helped her to stand.

"I am just going to put Thomas down in the cradle," she said softly. He nodded, but she saw concern in his eyes. He knew her too well.

She hurried up the stairs and into her bedchamber, slowing as she set Thomas down and covered him with a blanket. She stared at him, aware of how empty her arms felt—how lonely she was. She wanted the ease and laughter she had seen between Diana and Harry. But there had been nothing easy about the last couple years of marriage.

But was the loss she and Miles had experienced an inevitability? How many times had Miles tried to tease her, only to be met with polite responses that chilled any possibility of continuing the interaction? When had she begun to assume that his attempts to make her smile or be near her were simply masks for his desire to have an heir?

Quietly, she moved to the desk her mirror sat upon. A glass vial within rolled toward her. It lay atop the letter from the solicitor, but it had been there long before. She hadn't opened it yet except to smell it after first receiving it. The apothecary had told her it would help to bring on her courses. It had been months since she'd had them. At first, she had been hopeful that their disappearance was because she was pregnant. She hadn't told Miles—to do so would have felt like a repetition of what had happened at Christmas—and, in time, it became clear that she was *not* pregnant. There was none of the fatigue or sickness that had plagued her the first time, and there was no rounding of her belly as time went on.

Instead, she was left with the terrifying thought that she was well and truly barren now.

But the thought of partaking of the pennyroyal was just as terrifying. If it brought on her courses, she would have no excuse anymore. She had told herself that there was little purpose in sharing a bed with Miles if she couldn't conceive. It had been salve on her conscience and a bit of balm at the uncomfortable knowledge that she was not fulfilling her marital obligations.

But it was a feeble excuse, and she knew it well. If her courses returned, she would have to face the truth of things: she was afraid. She was afraid that she had lost Miles's love, that in her he saw only failure and regret. She was afraid that she could never make him happy and that, for him, the only purpose in sharing a bed *was* for the child he hoped it would lead to.

Near the back of the drawer, in the shadows, sat a seashell. She reached for it and pulled it into the light, rubbing a finger along its soft grooves. She had kept it on the desk in her room in Brighton all summer, but it had been sitting in the back of this drawer for years now.

She and Miles had collected many seashells together during their time in Brighton five years ago, but Lydia had kept only this one—the first one he gave her. She turned it, finding the little opening and smiling sadly and setting it to her ear. It was almost as if she could hear the memories of that sweet summer.

Was that all the happy times would ever be now? Memories in a drawer? Would she keep longing for the past and avoiding the present?

She eyed the pennyroyal again and set down the shell beside it, pulling the vial from the drawer. She uncorked the lid and took a quick sip before she could think better of it. She couldn't avoid things forever.

With a quick word to Jane to listen for Thomas, Lydia returned to the drawing room. The door was slightly ajar when she returned, the kissing bough twirling slowly from the top of the doorway. Within, Mary played a merry tune while Harry and Diana danced in a circle with arms linked, cheered on by the clapping of Robinson and Miles.

Lydia watched Miles, trying to remember what it had been like to see him five years ago, letting all of the hurt and disappointment and burdens of the more recent past fall like scales from her eyes. She could still see the way the Brighton wind swept the blond hair into his eyes as he'd led her and her sisters down the beach in search of more seashells.

She had been enamored of him, even knowing that he and Miss Kirkland were intended for each other. He had been so kind and attentive, not only to her, but to her sisters and parents, too. It had felt too good to be true—a dream from an idyllic world—when he had found reasons, day after day, to come to their townhouse and as she had seen suggestions of his regard for her in his eyes and behavior.

What had happened to change things so drastically from then to the way they were now?

Another twinge of longing settled deep within her, and, as if he had felt it, Miles turned toward her, followed by Robinson.

"She's here!" Robinson cried as Lydia opened the door to the drawing room and shut the door on her nostalgia.

Suddenly, Mary was pounding away on the piano, and all eyes were on Lydia. She blinked, trying to take stock of what was happening.

"Since you had to leave the room," Diana said loudly enough that she could be heard over the piano, "we thought you might as well be the next candidate for the game!"

"Oh!" Lydia laughed nervously and stepped fully into the room. She knew her sisters well enough to guess that they wouldn't forgo the opportunity to embarrass her. "Very well. Let's see...." She took a step nearer to Mary, and the volume increased. A step in the opposite direction brought the same result, so she stepped toward the sofa, and Mary played a bit softer.

Miles was looking at her with a strange expression on his face, and she looked a question at him. He almost seemed apologetic. No doubt he felt badly that she had been selected without any choice in the matter. The music grew louder, and Lydia realized she was standing in place.

She took another step toward the sofa and was rewarded with a less jarring string of chords. Was her object a person, yet again? She stood closer to Diana, and when the music amplified, her heart began to race. *Of course* her object was Miles. It was very much like Diana to scheme. Lydia may have been taking pains to put on a façade persuading her sisters that nothing was amiss in the marriage, but Diana was no fool.

The music softened to an almost imperceptible volume when Lydia stepped before her husband. And still, his eyes held apology in them, an apology that stung her conscience. Had she pushed him so very far from her that he felt he needed to apologize that she was obliged to come near him, even as part of a game?

She had found her object. Now what was the task required of her? They wouldn't have her repeat what had been done already by Robinson and Harry, and that was well enough, for she didn't think she could keep her composure if she were obliged to kneel before Miles and pretend it was all in good fun.

Was she to sit next to him? She tried, only to stop immediately at a crescendo in Mary's playing. Perhaps on his lap? How embarrassing. She put a hand on his knee and turned slightly to signify her intent, but no. That was not it. She put her hand out, and Miles took it, his gaze never leaving her face, as if he was trying to gauge how she was responding to all of this. She kept her mouth drawn in a smile, hoping it would reassure him. The music softened, and Miles rose from the sofa.

She tried various things with him beside her: curtsying to him, setting out her hands in preparation for a dance, and finally taking up his hand to walk the edge of the room. Perhaps they were meant to read a book together or snuff a candle. But they passed those objects with no significant change in Mary's playing.

She continued leading him, feeling almost as nervous as the first time he had taken her hand. What would their four spectators say to know that Lydia's heart hammered in her chest and her hands clung to her gloves in this moment? Or that, as the music softened at their approach to the door and her eyes caught sight of the kissing bough, her heart stopped altogether?

Every one of the others was laughing, but there was no humor in

Miles's eyes. Lydia tried to ignore her own nerves, which pummeled her from the inside, and she smiled at him. This was no great matter. They would share a quick kiss under the bough. It would appease the people watching them, and perhaps it would give Miles just a sliver of reassurance.

He tried to return her smile, but it was weak. Now that they had found their task, the music began to get louder again, as if Mary was intent on making them understand that they were meant to do more than just stand beneath the kissing bough.

Lydia strengthened her smile, but she felt the heat creeping into her cheeks as she went up on her tiptoes. She and Miles had always had to meet halfway to kiss—to bridge the distance between their disparate heights—until Lydia had slowly begun to let Miles traverse the entire distance himself. And then, one day, he had stopped trying at all.

He hesitated a moment, and she wondered with another stab of guilt whether he was remembering all the times she had rejected his attempts or met them with tight-lipped kisses. But he leaned down toward her, and their lips touched for the briefest of moments before parting again. Had he even closed his eyes? She rather thought not.

The music crescendoed again, and they were met with jeers and hisses.

Lydia's cheeks flamed, in part from how quickly Miles had pulled away, and in part from the reaction of their audience. "What?" she asked defensively.

"That was no kiss!" Harry said. "Come on, you two!"

"You can do better than that, surely," Robinson cried, and still the music played. Mary's hands must be exhausted by now.

Lydia looked at Miles, feeling entirely helpless. And yet there was a sense of thrill in the knowledge that a different kind of kiss was required of them. Robinson insisted they could do better. But she wasn't certain anymore.

CHAPTER 11

※

Miles had wanted to strangle his brother Harry on more than one occasion in his life, but never had he wished to so much as he did now. Harry had no idea what situation he had forced upon Miles, and Miles couldn't even send him a glance promising revenge to convey it. When the group had come up with the suggested object and task, Miles had lightly resisted it at first. But all his tentative comments had been thrust aside by Harry, leaving Miles with no other option than to assent, knowing that more reluctance on his part would raise questions neither he nor Lydia wanted raised.

After all, why in the world would a man be so reluctant to kiss his own wife?

Undoubtedly, Lydia would think that it was Miles himself who had suggested it, setting it down to his desperation for any kind of intimacy with her and his willingness to obtain it no matter what it required.

And the truth was, he *was* desperate. But he was desperate to return to a time when Lydia had willingly received his kisses, when she had happily initiated them and pulled him closer with a smile on her lips.

That Lydia had been gone for a long time now, though. And the thought of having to force yet another kiss upon her to appease their siblings and Robinson? He could only hope she would understand.

"Go on, then," Diana said. "It isn't as though we hadn't ever seen the two of you kiss before!"

Miles clenched his teeth tighter, while the blush on Lydia's cheeks deepened. There was no way out of it that he could see, unless they wished to appear strange—and seem like sticks in the mud.

Lydia was looking up at him, searching his eyes, and what he saw in hers held him in place. It was not reluctance or the wariness he had come to recognize so easily. It was uncertainty. His eyes trailed down to her lips, and he forced them back up. She offered a feeble smile, and it was enough to give him hope that perhaps she wouldn't hold this against him.

She closed her eyes and lifted her chin, and, with a thumping heartbeat, he shut his own eyes and leaned in, letting his lips find their way to hers, trying to forget that four people watched him kiss his wife for the first time in months.

The kiss was timid and gentle, so very different from the perfunctory ones which had finally persuaded him to stop even trying to kiss her not long after they had stopped sleeping in the same bedroom. Impulse told him to put his arms around Lydia's waist, but he refrained. He didn't want to do anything to ruin this moment.

Two hands came up to Miles's chest, holding onto the lapels of his coat and pulling him in toward her. Giving in gladly to the force, Miles wrapped one arm about Lydia's waist. With the other, cradled the back of her head, letting his lips explore hers, reveling in the simultaneous novelty and familiarity of the feeling, of the connection he had nearly given up on rekindling.

Clapping and whistling sounded, and they broke apart, Lydia averting her gaze as her cheeks immediately filled with color. She let her hands drop from his chest, and he reluctantly released her from his hold, his breath coming quickly and his mind racing.

"That's much more like it," Harry said with a wide grin as he clapped slowly.

Mary had her hands in her lap and was rubbing them. She had been playing for the better part of half an hour.

"Don't forget to take a berry," Diana said cheerfully.

Miles glanced at Lydia, who smiled shyly at him and looked up at the kissing bough. He reached up for the nearest berry and plucked it off, offering it to Lydia. She took it and, with another glance at Miles, turned toward their company.

❄

Try as he might, Miles had been unable to keep his eyes from his wife for the duration of the evening. He had so many questions, and perhaps if he looked at her often enough, he would find the answer there. Only during dinner, when she was seated to his side, did he manage to refrain from looking at her and then simply because to do so would be too obvious.

The question that kept repeating in his mind like the chiming of a clock on the hour was *what in the world just happened?* He might have believed he had imagined the entire thing if it weren't for the fact that he could still feel the tingling of his lips whenever he thought on the kiss. He could remember, too, how it felt to have Lydia pulling him toward her. How could he ever forget it?

What did it mean, though? What had changed? Or were they to return to the way things had been for the past year, mere passing ships in the house they lived in together?

Lydia's gaze met his a number of times over the course of the night, and whenever it did, there was a pensive look about her that Miles would have given anything to have interpreted for him. Did she regret it? Had it just been to appease the company there?

It was with a racing heart that Miles scaled the stairs with Lydia and her sisters after Harry's and Robinson's departure. It might be foolish of him to expect anything different tonight, but—heaven help him—he couldn't stop himself. Diana and Mary bid them goodnight, continuing on their way down the corridor toward their own bedchambers, while Lydia and Miles stopped in front of Miles's door.

There was silence between them as they watched the sisters disappear through their respective doors, and then, as if at the snap of two fingers, the air thickened.

Lydia looked up at him, and he smiled at her, hoping to set her at ease.

"I think that was rather successful," he said.

"I think so too. Both Mary and Diana seemed to enjoy themselves."

"Harry and Robinson, too, which is significant, as they think themselves above most simple entertainments these days," he said dryly.

She laughed, and more silence followed. He wanted to invite her into his room to continue discussing the evening—he was reluctant to end their time together—but he was still too unsure what had happened between them under the kissing bough to face the rejection he avoided at all costs these days.

Her gaze flitted to the door behind him, and she opened her mouth, only to be interrupted.

"My lady," said Jane, holding Thomas in her arms and a bottle in one hand. His face was red and unhappy. "You said you wished me to bring him to you when it was time to feed him before sleep?"

Lydia glanced at Miles then smiled at Jane, putting out her hands to receive him. "Yes, of course."

Thomas fussed and wriggled.

"Oh dear." Lydia took the prepared bottle from Jane. "Very ornery, aren't you? There, there, my dear. Let us get something in that belly of yours. Thank you, Jane. You may go."

Jane curtsied and left them, while Thomas writhed and flailed his arms, his whining turning into cries.

Lydia looked at Miles with a sort of grimace. "I should go feed him."

He nodded quickly, hoping it hid his disappointment. "Of course." He took one of Thomas's hands and shook it lightly. He didn't know whether to kiss the baby or curse him. Lydia had changed for the better with Thomas's arrival, but the baby certainly had little respect for Miles's wishes. "Goodnight, little chap."

Lydia hesitated for a moment as though she might say something, but Thomas would have none of it. "Goodnight, Miles," she said.

"Goodnight, Lydia." He stifled a sigh and opened the door to his room.

CHAPTER 12

JANUARY 1810

Lydia winced as she pulled the brush through her hair, sitting before the mirror. "Ouch," she said, setting down the brush and exploring the knotted mess with a frown. Her fingers met with something cold, and she paused. She had missed a pin. She extracted it, sighed, and picked up the brush again.

"Where is Sarah?" Miles asked as his valet left the room.

"I gave her the night off," Lydia responded.

She saw Miles cringe sympathetically as her brush snagged yet again.

"Can I try?" He came up behind her, and Lydia met his gaze through the mirror, her own questioning. He put out a hand for the brush. "I promise I shall be gentle."

She surrendered the brush to him, and he took a section of her hair in hand.

"I think you must start brushing from the bottom," he said, doing just that.

She raised a brow at him, and he seemed to sense it, since he looked up and laughed at the sight of her expression. "What? I used to watch my mother sometimes."

"I know very well how to brush hair," Lydia said. "I am merely impatient. And perhaps out of practice as well." She had brushed her own hair growing up. It was only when she'd had her coming out that her mother had insisted she allow a maid to see to her hair.

Miles managed to pull the brush all the way from the roots to the ends, and she closed her eyes. Her head was aching from her coiffure, and the feel of the bristles against her scalp relieved some of the itching. Miles repeated the motion a few more times then set aside that section, starting on another.

"Perhaps I should be employing you rather than Sarah," Lydia said with a teasing smile.

Miles lifted his shoulders. "I wouldn't mind taking on this part of her duties. It is somewhat relaxing, in truth. Besides"—he moved the section of hair to the side and leaned down to kiss the part of her neck it revealed—"I would never say no to more time with you."

Her skin tingled where his lips had been, and she turned her head up to look at him. What other husband offered to brush his wife's hair every night? She put her hand to his cheek and pulled him toward her for a long, deep kiss.

❉

The Present

Lydia watched Thomas's lashes flutter and close, only to open again for a moment, droop, shut, and repeat. He was fighting sleep, but the calming of the bottle he was drinking seemed to be quickly winning out, and his eyelids finally closed more firmly.

She glanced at the door connecting her room to Miles's and stared at it thoughtfully. She still wasn't certain whether to be glad or regretful over what had happened in the corridor. She had wondered for a moment if Miles might invite her into his bedchamber after their kiss—and at the realization that she didn't know whether she wished for or dreaded it. Her emotions were in a tangle, and she hardly knew what she wanted anymore.

With their kiss, hope had burgeoned within her. She had certainly initiated the kiss, but Miles had returned it with a fervor that had set her on fire—but brought on a sliver of misgiving in retrospect. How could she want his affection so desperately while also fearing it? She wanted reassurance that he didn't regret marrying her, that he didn't wish he had married Miss Kirkland, and the kiss had felt like just that.

But perhaps she had misinterpreted it. Perhaps it was another instance of the very thing she had spent the last few months avoiding: evidence of his wish for a return to intimacy between them, a persistent hope that she could still give him an heir.

She clamped her eyes shut, aggravated with herself and the complete mess she was in. The hesitancy and apology she had seen in Miles's eyes earlier? How could that possibly come as a surprise? She confused *herself* with how back and forth she was in her thoughts and feelings—of course he would be confused as well.

She rose from the chair and went to place Thomas in his cradle. She was still in her evening dress, her hair still coiffed. It was only in the last year that she had called for her maid at night. Before that, Miles had helped her undo the fastenings on whatever dress she was wearing and then brushed out her hair.

Lydia felt the familiar pang of longing then went and pulled the bell for Sarah.

❄

Miles was not at the breakfast table at the normal hour the next morning, and it wasn't until Diana and Mary descended from their rooms later on that he returned, cheeks and nose red from the cold and a wide smile on his face.

"It is far too early for anyone to look so odiously joyful," Diana said teasingly.

"Early?" he responded. "You have missed the better half of the day already."

Diana took the cup of tea Lydia poured. "The better half? Hardly. Nothing of note happens before the afternoon."

"Well," Miles said, snatching up a roll from the table, "today that may well be true, but only because, unlike you, I didn't stay abed."

Lydia looked at him through narrowed eyes, letting Thomas chomp on her finger. "What do you mean?"

He only grinned. "It will be better as a surprise. All I can say is to dress warmly once you've breakfasted."

Lydia searched his face for any sign of what he was concealing, but without success. "Is this secret activity safe for the likes of this little one?" She clapped Thomas's slobbery hands together, and his mouth stretched into a smile full of gums.

Miles looked at him consideringly. "I cannot see why he should not join with us."

"Will it be too cold for him, do you think?"

Miles crouched down and made a dramatic frown. "You dare doubt the strength of the mighty Thomas?" He pulled the baby's arms up in a victorious pose. "He spent an evening in naught but a blanket at the Frost Fair, and he seems none the worse for it."

Lydia gave him a censuring look. "I doubt he wishes to repeat the experience."

Miles let Thomas's hands drop. "Well, then, it will all depend upon how tightly he can abide being bundled, won't it?"

They left the townhouse at two o'clock, everyone wearing their warmest coats, gloves, and scarves. Miles laughed at the sight of Thomas, whom Lydia and Jane had swaddled in no fewer than three blankets.

"Is there truly a baby in there?" Miles asked, coming over to peer down at the bundle in Lydia's arms.

Wide eyes looked up at them amidst the blankets.

"We are to go on an adventure, Thomas," Miles said. "Here, let me hold him. We have a bit of a walk before us."

Lydia complied, looking through narrowed eyes at her husband. "Where *are* we going?"

He only wagged his brows enigmatically and signaled with a tip of the head for her to follow him. He was at his most charming when he had a secret, and Lydia couldn't help feeling intrigued by his energy.

Down the cold street, the five of them walked, avoiding patches of ice and dirty snow, while a few snowflakes drifted down lazily from the sky. They were heading in the direction of the Park, and as they passed under the gates, a little gasp came from Diana.

"What is it?" Mary asked, trying to follow the direction of her sister's gaze.

Diana pointed. "Are those for us, Miles?"

Two red sleighs, both pulled by a pair of matched horses and attended by men in dark great coats, stood on the snow.

"Maybe," he said, but his smile was answer enough.

"A sleigh ride?" Lydia asked, blinking.

A hint of uncertainty crept into Miles's eyes as he looked down at her. "Yes. Is that all right?"

She laughed. "Don't be ridiculous, Miles. I have always wished to ride in a sleigh."

"I know," he replied.

Diana and Mary were already scurrying toward the second sleigh, and the driver assisted them into their seats, leaving Miles, Lydia, and Thomas to share the first one. Thomas was fidgeting, seemingly unhappy with having such limited use of his arms, and Lydia pulled off the outermost—and thickest—blanket so she could sit him on her lap, giving him the chance to look around. He blinked as a stray snowflake landed on his eyelash, and Miles laughed and brushed it away.

"Anywhere in particular you wish to go, my lord?" asked the driver.

Miles settled into his seat. "Take us wherever you would wish to go yourself."

The man gave a nod. "I like that answer, my lord. And what pace would you prefer? Gentle or quick?"

Miles looked at Lydia, and she raised her brows. "Why not a bit of both?" he said.

Another nod from the driver, a flick of the reins, and the sleigh pulled forward.

Thomas had been watching the snowflakes, reaching out for some that were far too distant for him to touch, but at the moving of the sleigh, his characteristic wide-eyed expression appeared, one of his hands still suspended in the air, his face frozen in alarm.

Miles covered his mouth, but his shoulders shook. "Our little winter statue." He pushed down with a finger on the baby's arm, and it popped right back into place.

Lydia swatted at Miles's hand. "He is not a statue. He is merely showing the appropriate awe for such a scene." She looked around and felt a similar amazement fill her. The Park was hardly recognizable, enveloped in a blanket of snow that sparkled as she let her eyes follow the drifts they passed.

"It *is* quite a sight, isn't it?" Miles said in a soft voice.

The sleigh suddenly picked up speed, and the cold air whipped at their faces. Lydia turned a shocked Thomas in toward her, laughing as falling snow stuck to her cheeks and nose.

"Here," Miles said, sliding his arm around behind her, and she nestled into the empty space, turning her body and face toward him, glad that her smile was covered. The feeling of being close to Miles was even better than she had remembered it.

As the sleigh charged forward, Lydia noticed for the first time the clinking of the bells attached to the collars around the horses' necks. They jingled especially loudly as the sleigh bumped over a stretch of uneven ground, eliciting a delicious giggle from Thomas and a glance of shared delight between Lydia and Miles.

Sliding through a wonderland of white, warmed by Miles's arm cradled around her, and with a laughing baby on her lap, Lydia thought she might be living a bit of heaven in that moment.

❄

Dark was falling as they made their way home from the Park, but merriment prevailed despite the chill air that had begun to seep through their clothing and cause their noses to run. Diana and Mary finished the last stanza of a Christmas carol as they passed over the threshold of the townhouse and began pulling off their bonnets and wool pelisses to hand to the footman.

"Oh heavens," said Mary with a hand to her hair. "The wind has not been kind to my coiffure."

"No, it has not," Diana said, trying without success to stifle a laugh as she looked at Mary.

"Yours is hardly better, I think." Mary plucked the bonnet off Diana's head and laughed at the sight.

Lydia let Miles take the sleeping Thomas as she pulled off her own bonnet and felt the shocking disarray of her hair. "Only Miles and Thomas have escaped unscathed, I think."

Mary let out a large sigh. "What a mess it will be to brush through."

"Yes, well," Diana said, "it will have to wait until bedtime, for I cannot abide another moment in this state of starvation. You don't mind if we stay in these clothes, do you, Miles? I must say, the sleigh ride was a stroke of genius, but would it be a vain hope that you also had the foresight to set dinner forward?"

Lydia glanced at him with an eyebrow raised in teasing challenge.

"Oh, ye of little faith," he said. "Can you not even now smell the delights in store for you?"

Diana and Mary gave a couple of sniffs, and their eyes widened. "Do I detect goose?"

Miles gave a formal nod. "Is that acceptable to you?"

Diana only laughed. "Hurry on, then, everyone!"

Miles surrendered Thomas to Jane, who had a bottle in hand, prepared for the moment he woke, and Lydia went in to dinner on Miles's arm.

There was never more than a moment of quiet with Diana in company, and the four of them made quick work of the food Cook had prepared for their consumption, reflecting on the happenings of the day and debating how long the current cold weather would last.

"Well," said Diana on a sigh once they were all sitting back in their seats, satisfied with the meal. "I suppose after an entire day in our company, Miles might like some time alone to enjoy his port. And that is for the best, I think, for I mean to go straight upstairs and set to untangling this web." She made an expression of distaste as she put a hand to her hair.

Mary followed suit and gave a resigned sigh. "I should never have removed my bonnet, but the wind was pulling it so much, I thought the ribbons might strangle me. I may need your help brushing through it, Di." She glanced at Diana and narrowed her eyes. "No, never mind. I'd rather have Lydia. She has a softer touch."

Diana's mouth dropped open in offense. "What utter nonsense! I am *very* gentle."

Lydia stifled a smile and shared a significant look with Mary.

"Tell her it is untrue, Lydia," Diana said, looking at her expectantly.

Lydia took her lips between her teeth and gave a little shake of the head. "I am sorry, Di. Of the three of us, you certainly have the least regard for tender heads."

"Well!" Diana tossed her napkin onto the table. "See if I ever help any of you again!" She glanced at Miles, and a twinkle entered her eye. "I don't mean you, Miles. Naturally, I would be more than happy to brush out your hair if you ever required my help."

Miles put two hands on his head in a defensive gesture. "Please, no. My head is even more tender than Lydia's."

"It is true," Lydia said. "And I think it is why he has such gentle hands himself. If I was forced to choose someone in this room to untangle my hair, it would certainly be Miles."

Diana and Mary both raised their brows, and Lydia nodded. "He has a fair bit of skill with hair."

"You unman me, my dear," he replied with a twitch at the corner of his mouth.

"I changed my mind," Diana said, pushing back her chair and rising. "You shall not linger over your port, Miles. You shall be occupied for the time being, demonstrating this supposed hidden talent."

"Is that right?" Miles asked.

"It is."

Miles looked to Lydia, who only shrugged with a smile. Once Diana was set on something, it was difficult to turn her from it. Besides, Miles was certainly capable of finding an excuse to avoid the suggested activity if he truly had a mind to.

"Don't dawdle, now," Diana said. "We have quite a bit of hair between the three of us."

Miles let out a snort, but he rose from his seat. "You expect me to spend the rest of the evening acting as lady's maid to all of you, I take it?"

"It is good for you, Miles," Diana said. "If you *do* have such skill with hair, it must be practiced and refined, or you shall lose it altogether, and I couldn't bear that."

Lydia met Miles's dry gaze with a bit of shyness. He *hadn't* had the opportunity to practice recently.

They made their way upstairs, and Diana insisted they go in Miles's room. "For I have no doubt at all that Lydia's brushes are superior to mine. I have your old ones, you know."

Lydia glanced nervously at Miles, but his face was impassive. Her brushes weren't *in* the room Diana expected them to be in.

"Did you not ask Sarah to clean your brushes this morning?" Miles asked.

Lydia stared at him for a moment. She hadn't asked anything of the sort, and even if she had, he wouldn't have known. But suddenly, she understood. He was trying to help her. "Yes, I did."

"Hopefully she is done," Miles said as they reached the door to his bedchamber. "I could never abide using the inferior sort of brushes Diana claims hers are." He winked at Lydia.

"I shall just go see, then," Lydia said, and she held back while Diana and Mary followed Miles into the room.

She hurried to her own bedchamber and into her room, grabbing the brushes and combs sitting upon the table in front of the mirror then hurrying back to Miles's room.

"Ah, wonderful," Diana said, coming over and taking the large brush from her. "You can start with Lydia's hair, Miles. Something you're familiar with. And proof of your skill before I allow you to touch *my* hair." She frowned at the brush in her hand. "I thought you said Sarah was going to clean these." She rubbed at a spot on the back.

"Oh," Lydia said with a flutter of nerves, "she must not have had time to get to them."

"No matter," Diana said. "Come, have a seat. Here, Miles." She handed him the brush. "Get to work, then, *maestro*." She and Mary sat on the bed to observe.

Lydia took a seat on the chair in front of the mirror, feeling a sudden rush of nerves. For months, she and Miles had shared no intimate interactions at all, and now that Diana and Mary and Thomas were here, they were being thrust into situation after situation where more was required of them. She didn't know what to feel about any of it.

Miles came behind her, and they met eyes in the mirror briefly, his gaze searching her face with a nervousness to match her own. He set the brush down and put a hand to her head in search of the pins holding up her hair. He pulled gently at one, and a lock of hair fell down, the end slipping into the back of her dress. He placed a finger behind the hair to pull it out, and Lydia's skin trembled, a shiver running down her spine.

"At this rate," Diana said, crossing her arms, "we shall be here until tomorrow evening."

Miles let out a chuckle and set to taking out the rest of the pins. "I think I shall decline the honor of tending to *your* hair, Diana, grievous as the thought is to me."

"Why do you think Diana does her own hair?" Mary said teasingly. "She could never find a maid who did it to her satisfaction, so Mother finally threw up her hands and told her to do it herself."

Miles looked at Lydia, who confirmed it with a subtle nod, trying not to pay attention to the way his stabilizing hand felt on her head as he began to pull the brush through. He truly did have a gentle hand, and it had been so long since she had felt it. She missed their evenings together, talking and laughing. Not until now had she realized how lonely she had been for the last year.

More than a year, really. The distance between them had been creeping up for some time before things had come to a head with the loss of last Christmas—and the fight which had led to them sleeping separately not long after. She had felt such relief at not having to worry about failing expectation or crushing Miles's hopes of becoming pregnant that sleeping apart had been a relief to her. But, at some point, that relief that begun to feel more like loneliness.

Had he been feeling lonely too? Or was he merely regretful that he had ever decided to marry her at all?

"You *are* gentle," Diana said, coming to a stand, "but it is certainly at the cost of efficiency." She put out a hand for the brush and set it on the bed while she pulled the pins from her own coiffure. "Watch." With a ruthlessness that made Lydia wince, she ran the brush through her hair.

Miles, too, was drawing back, and the scandalized look on his face made Lydia's shoulders shake with laughter.

Mary sent them both a significant look. "Lydia," she said, "you *will* help me brush through mine if I need it, won't you?"

"Of course," Lydia said.

Miles turned back to Lydia and set to the task of plaiting her hair. "I am surprised you have any hair left, Diana."

There was a knock on the door, and Mary went to open it.

"Lydia," she called over. "Jane has brought Thomas."

"Come in, Jane," Lydia called.

"I'm sorry to disturb you, my lady." Jane bounced Thomas in her arms as she walked. "But the babe has been fussy, and he is beginning to feel a bit warm."

Lydia turned, forcing Miles to drop her hair. Thomas's cheeks were pink, and he fussed, brushing his fist against his nose.

"His nose has been running," Jane said. "At first I thought it was just from being outside, but it hasn't stopped, and I wonder if he is perhaps getting a cold."

Lydia clenched her teeth and looked at Miles. "It was thoughtless of me to take him out with us today." She put her arms out for Thomas. "Come here, my child. Let me see you. Thank you, Jane. Will you go get him another bottle? Just in case?"

The maid curtsied and left.

"Poor little man," Mary said with a sympathetic glance at Thomas. "We should leave them, Di."

Diana agreed, and they said goodnight and left the room shortly.

Lydia tipped Thomas so that he was lying in her arms then bounced him gently, noting his rosy cheeks, the little drip coming from his nose, and his overbright eyes.

Miles put a hand on her shoulder. "You mustn't blame yourself. He is a strong little boy. He will be well soon enough."

She swallowed, hoping he was right. "I am going to see if I can get him to sleep."

Miles nodded once, a bit of regret in his eyes.

She hesitated a moment. "Goodnight, Miles."

CHAPTER 13

MAY 1814

Miles rolled over to his other side for what felt like the thousandth time that night. He opened his eyes, heavy with fatigue but further from sleep than ever, and they settled on the empty spot beside him.

It had been weeks since Lydia had moved her things to the adjoining room. In the beginning, while her things had still remained in his bedchamber, he had thought the new sleeping situation was only temporary. They both needed a bit of time apart—to cool down and reflect upon the things they'd said to one another in their anger. But, night after night, Lydia had slept in the next room, and soon enough, her maid, Sarah, was moving her things there.

Miles shut his eyes against the remembered feelings of humiliation. What had Sarah thought of it all? He hated that the servants knew things were not well between him and Lydia.

It was ridiculous, though—them sleeping apart. They had always slept together, from the very beginning of their marriage. And Miles still wanted to. Even if Lydia didn't wish for the type of intimacy they *had used to share, he still wanted her beside him. Did she doubt that? Was that why she had stayed in the other room after all this time?*

The thought made him sit up and toss the bedcovers away from him. He rubbed his eyes, and his bleary gaze settled on the door to Lydia's room. He chewed his lip then rose to his feet, walking quietly over to it, where he paused.

What was he doing? It was the middle of the night. Lydia would be sleeping. It was no time for the discussion he wanted to have with her. And yet, he couldn't relax. He hadn't been sleeping well since their fight, and the thought of spending the rest of the night tossing and turning?

Perhaps he could just see if she was truly asleep. If she was, he would return to his bed and wait to talk to her until the day dawned. But maybe—just maybe—she was as restless as he was.

He put a hand on the doorknob and pushed. It didn't budge, and his stomach clenched.

She had locked it.

❆

The Present

Thomas was indeed sick, as was evidenced by the muffled crying Miles could hear coming from the neighboring bedroom when he woke in the morning. Had the baby cried all night? Or had he simply woken unhappy?

Miles threw off the bedcovers and glanced in the mirror, running a hand through his disheveled hair. He wrapped his dressing gown around himself and walked over to the door leading to Lydia's room, hesitating a moment then tapping softly.

Fool. She couldn't hear such a knock over the sound of Thomas's crying. He put a hand toward the door knob, and it hovered there for a moment before settling upon it. He pulled it gently, and it opened. Not locked, then. Somehow, that was comforting to him. Whether she had forgotten to relock it or had left it unlocked on purpose was the question. He had checked it enough times over the past few months to know that it was kept locked as a rule.

He opened the door wider and looked inside.

"Shh, shh," Lydia was saying as she bounced up and down, wearing only her chemise, which had slipped over one of her shoulders. "It will all be all right, my love." She kissed the side of Thomas's head, and Miles swallowed at the sight, at the nurturing that came so naturally to his wife.

The door creaked, and she looked over. He pushed it open. "I'm sorry. I didn't mean to—I heard him crying and thought I would see if I could do anything to help."

She smiled weakly. "It is very kind of you. I admit my arms are beginning to tire."

He walked over and took the baby. "Has he been this way all night? I must have slept very soundly if so." He had certainly *not* slept soundly, but nor had he heard Thomas crying.

"You always do," she said. "But no, he actually slept quite well. He woke for a little while during the night, but he just wanted to be held, so I brought him in the bed with me."

Lucky devil.

"He woke very unhappy, though," she continued, "and the rocking is the only thing that seems to keep him somewhat calm. Jane should be bringing a bottle for him soon."

"You like being rocked, do you?" Miles asked a whining Thomas. "Just how *much* do you like it?" He swayed back and forth energetically, and Thomas went quiet, his widening eyes giving way to a little smile.

"Ah," Miles said, "so you prefer dramatics to subtlety. Well, then." He spun around, dipping and rising, and Thomas cooed then giggled while Lydia looked on, smiling.

Miles let his movements take him over to Lydia, where he stopped and tipped up Thomas so he could smile at her. "Now you know what he wishes for you to do all day. A small request, I think."

She chuckled and tapped Thomas on the nose. "I haven't the stamina for such a thing, I'm afraid."

Soon, both Thomas's smiles and cries disappeared as he set to the task of consuming his bottle, at the completion of which activity, he was fast asleep. Miles held him while he slept, but when Thomas woke an hour later, he was as unhappy as ever and continued to be so for the duration of the day. Diana and Mary seemed unconcerned with the prospect of a day at home, given the temperature of the air outside, which had dipped again. Only those who couldn't avoid doing so seemed to be out and about in Town.

Lydia, Jane, and Cook spent a great deal of the day trying different things to soothe the increasingly miserable Thomas, and by the time everyone was turning in for bed, the baby was refusing to sleep or take a bottle at all.

"Let me take him," Miles said. "You must be exhausted."

Lydia shook her head. "A little tired is all. Perhaps you could give him his bottle while I prepare for bed, though. Then I can take him again."

Miles obliged, and he took Thomas into his bedchamber, choosing a spot on the bed rather than the chair beside it. "For I am determined that Lydia shall let me keep you for a bit," he said to Thomas. "You have been wearing her out all day, you know."

To Miles's surprise, Thomas accepted the bottle hungrily, and his complaining transformed into murmurs as his fingers toyed with the hand Miles used to hold the bottle and his eyes stared fixedly at Miles's face.

Miles returned the stare, admiring the large blue eyes that looked up at him above fevered cheeks. He hadn't had many opportunities to be alone with Thomas, and the contentment he felt surprised him. It was more than contentment, though.

Thomas's fingers wrapped tightly around Miles's thumb, and he stopped sucking on the bottle for a moment, smiling as the mixture of water, bread, and milk dripped into his mouth.

Miles smiled back at him, feeling the moment in his heart.

"Come on, chap. You're dripping." He moved the bottle slightly, and Thomas set back to eating, while Miles tried to swallow down the unexpected emotion.

It wasn't long before Thomas had drained the glass bottle of its contents, and he made no secret of the fact that he was displeased about it. Miles tried to bounce him from his position on the bed, but the baby would have none of it, and he was working himself up to a frenzy when Lydia entered through the connecting door. She wore a wrapper over her shift, and her hair had been brushed but not plaited.

"He must still be hungry," Miles said, indicating the empty bottle.

Lydia came and sat down on the edge of the bed with a frown. "He goes from refusing it to draining it. Here, let me take him. You need to prepare for bed."

Miles felt double reluctance. He liked holding Thomas, and giving him up meant saying goodnight to Lydia, as well. They hadn't had any time at all during the course of the day to touch on any of the things that had happened in the past few days, and anytime Miles thought about it, he felt he might go mad wondering what it all meant.

But he surrendered Thomas to her, all the same. He was afraid of bringing up the subject. If he said something to her—asked her the questions he had—he might well face rejection. At least now, he had some hope. Perhaps it was better to hold onto that than risk it.

"I could take him for a part of the night," he suggested.

"I hope it shan't be necessary. If I can only get him to sleep, he may do well enough." She smiled at Miles as Thomas's cries heightened. "Goodnight, then."

"Goodnight," he said, watching as the two of them left his room. In many ways, his relationship with Lydia had improved since Thomas's arrival. But, in other ways, he felt Lydia was farther from him than ever. It was as if she was in her own little world when she was alone with Thomas.

Miles could hear the baby's crying through the walls as his valet helped him out of his clothes, and he determined to go to Lydia and insist on helping after his valet left. But the cries had grown fainter by then.

He listened for a moment then slipped into bed. But he tossed and turned, unable to keep his mind from everything that was happening, unable to stop his ears from straining to hear what might be happening in Lydia's room.

At some point, he fell asleep, but it was a restless sleep, and when he woke more fully, by the light of the fire in his room, he could see on his pocketwatch that it was just shy of midnight.

He stilled. Thomas was crying again. Perhaps that was what had roused him. He slid out of bed, pulling on his dressing gown as he went to the door to Lydia's room and opened it.

Lydia looked up at his entrance, bouncing up and down in her chemise with a hint of desperation in her eyes. "He is miserable," she said. "He hasn't slept at all yet, but he won't take a bottle, and he is so terribly tired."

"Why did you not come for me?" Miles said, sliding his hands under the blanket Thomas was in so that he could take him from Lydia. His crying turned to frustrated grunting at the disturbance.

Lydia tipped him into Miles's arms and shrugged. She looked exhausted. "I didn't want to disturb you."

He cradled Thomas in one arm and put a hand on Lydia's cheek. "You were never meant to do this all on your own, Lydia. Let me share in it with you. That is what I am here for."

She put her hand over his and shut her eyes. "You shouldn't have to sacrifice your sleep. It was my idea to bring him home with us."

"And I am very glad for it. He is a light in this house."

Her hand dropped from his as she sighed.

"I *want* to help, Lydia. I want to share in both the burden and the joy."

She looked at him intently for a moment then nodded and looked down at Thomas. "He is less fussy with you."

He gave a wry smile. "It is only the novelty. But we should capitalize on the silence. Will you hand me the bottle?"

She gave it to him, and he put it to Thomas's lips. He fussed, but Miles persisted, and Thomas finally took it.

Miles took two steps backward to sit on the edge of Lydia's bed, and she followed him there with a sigh of relief. "Thank heaven."

They both watched the baby as he ate, Lydia leaning in on Miles's shoulder for a better view. Every now and then, they shared a look of amusement or appreciation as Thomas made the sounds and expressions that were so particular to him. When his eyes finally shut and he stopped drinking, Miles gave the mostly-empty bottle to Lydia.

"Don't move," she whispered urgently as she set the bottle down. "You might wake him."

Miles opened his mouth then shut it. He was to sit here all night, then? Perhaps that wouldn't be so bad. "You should at least sleep while he sleeps," he said.

She stared at Thomas thoughtfully. "I *am* quite tired. But..." She pursed her lips. "It doesn't feel right for me to sleep while you sit there like that."

"What," he said with a smile, "like I just slept while you rocked him for hours?" He nodded at the bed behind him. "Lie down. Rest your eyes. I will see to Thomas. And wake you if I need you."

She chewed her lip for a moment then assented, walking around to the other side of the bed. There was a great deal of uncertainty in her movements as she pulled back the bedcovers and climbed in. Of course, it must be strange for her to have him there in this room where he had never before slept, watching her. She lay down, turning on her left side so that she faced away from him. That alone let him know that all of it was slightly uncomfortable for her—she always slept on her right side.

He found himself rocking gently from side to side, even though Thomas was fast asleep for the time being. He had no idea how much time had passed by the time Lydia's breathing slowed and deepened, but it finally did.

He looked pensively at Thomas, at the rise and fall of his chest and the pout of his lower lip. His back was beginning to ache from sitting upright, and he glanced at the empty space on the bed next to him, beside Lydia. Perhaps he could move slowly and carefully enough to rest his back against the headboard, at least.

He waited for a moment, debating, then shifted his position, eyes flitting rapidly between Thomas and Lydia to verify that neither of them were being disturbed by the adjustment. They both slept soundly.

Slowly but surely, Miles moved from his place at the edge of the bed toward the headboard, finally lifting his feet and setting them on top of the blanket. He sighed with contented relief at the ability to rest his body against something solid. Only one more thing, and he could be perfectly comfortable. Well, not perfectly comfortable, but sufficiently so.

He took two spare pillows, setting one beneath the elbow that cradled Thomas and one in front of his arm to keep Thomas from rolling away in the event that Miles's hold slackened. Then he shut his eyes and let his head fall back.

This was much better. He might even get some sleep this way. He hoped Lydia wouldn't mind if she woke to see him thus.

She stirred beside him and, with a puckered brow, turned on her back then to her right side, bringing a smile to Miles's lips. He allowed himself a moment to admire her face. Heavens, but she was beautiful when she was so relaxed and at peace. Her hair was strung about, never having been plaited, and he resisted the impulse to touch it. How long had it been since he had seen her sleep from so near?

Again, Miles wasn't aware of when he fell asleep, but when he woke, it was to an awful ache in his neck and the realization that he had slipped down into a near-lying position, chin resting heavily on his chest. He hurriedly glanced at Thomas, who still slept soundly in his arms.

Miles shifted his arm a bit and winced at the pain. He couldn't stay like this. He eyed the cradle next to the bed. He couldn't just set Thomas in there and leave. But he could set him in there and lie beside him in case he stirred.

He shifted until he sat on the edge of the bed, clenching his teeth together with anxiety, then set Thomas in the cradle. He let out a large breath when his efforts met with success then shifted to look at Lydia.

She was still in the same position, one hand tucked under her cheek. He wished he could lay beside her. He needn't even get close enough to touch her. Just to know that she was there.

He sighed and pushed himself slowly from the bed. It creaked slightly, and Lydia stirred, her eyelids fluttering slightly. Miles froze in place, hovering just above the bed.

Lydia's eyes opened slightly, and her mouth pulled into a smile. Was she smiling at the sight of him? She couldn't be.

She shut her eyes and reached a lazy hand out toward him, as though waiting for him to take it. His heart thudded against his chest, and in a halting movement, he stretched his arm toward her, letting his fingers touch her hand. Her fingers wrapped around his hand, and she pulled him toward her.

Alarmed but not wishing to wake her by resisting, he lowered himself back onto the bed and allowed himself to be pulled nearer, being as careful not to make too much noise as he slid into the bed beside her. Was she at all conscious of what she was doing? If she wasn't and she woke to find him next to her....

He swallowed nervously.

"You got him to sleep," she said with a tired smile.

"Yes," he said. She was clearly somewhat aware of what she was doing, but he was still afraid that, if he spoke more, he might break whatever spell this was.

"Thank you, my love."

His heart stuttered, and it was with a crack in his voice that he responded, "You are welcome. My love." Her words gave him a spurt of courage, and he leaned in and set a soft kiss on her forehead. Only with the slightest quirk of her mouth did she betray that she even noticed, and then her breathing deepened, and she was soon asleep again.

Miles stayed up for some time, turned toward her, watching the steady rise and fall of her chest. He was afraid that, if he fell asleep, he might wake to discover it was all a dream.

How had he managed to sleep without her this past year? And how would he ever sleep without her again?

CHAPTER 14

❄

NOVEMBER 1812

Lydia breathed a sigh of relief to see Miles already in bed when she returned from the party she had attended. She didn't want to talk about her evening, and she hadn't the energy for the type of interaction Miles was no doubt expecting.

Sarah helped her undress in silence, and Lydia kept her eyes on Miles. He didn't stir, though, and Lydia dismissed her maid, brushed out her own hair, and plaited it.

Miles had attended a gathering with some of his fellow peers, while Lydia had felt obliged to at least show her face at a party they had been invited to. Unexpectedly, she had seen Sophia Kirkland there —or Lady Venton now, rather. Her glowing face and the barest hint of a rounding below the bodice of the dress she wore had made Lydia sick with envy. It was Lady Venton's second child. Lydia knew because her mother-in-law had made a point of telling Miles as much while Lydia was in the room.

Lydia sighed and crept quietly into bed, facing away from Miles and wincing with every sound the frame and mattress made. Miles stirred, turning toward her and reaching an arm out, and his hand came to rest on her arm. She waited to see if he would say anything, but it seemed he was still asleep. The warmth of his hand on her arm brought on a stinging in her eyes.

She suddenly felt the overwhelming desire to be held. It had been a difficult night, and she had faced it alone. Against her better judgment, she scooted back toward Miles so that his arm slid forward and around her waist. She grasped at it and tried to quell the tears that came. She didn't want Miles to see her cry, didn't want to answer the questions he would have. She was embarrassed of how insecure she had come to feel whenever Lady Venton made an appearance in their lives.

But, even more than that, she didn't want to rouse him because of what might happen next. The physician they had seen a few months ago had instructed them how long after the start of her courses would be most conducive to conceiving, and today marked the first of those days this month.

It was the last thing she wanted to do.

Miles's embrace tightened around her, and he moved closer. She tried not to stiffen. It was madness that she had to fight such an impulse. It had not always been so.

"You were out late," he said sleepily, his warm breath grazing the back of her neck.

"Yes," she said softly, hoping he might fall back asleep if she didn't say any more.

But his breath on her neck turned to kisses, and she clenched her eyes shut. This was what she wanted, wasn't it? They both did. They wanted a child. An heir.

So why had it become such a burden to be shown affection—and to return it?

❄

The Present

Thomas was fussing in the room somewhere, but Lydia couldn't see anything. It was mostly dark, but for a flickering of flames in the fireplace. She frowned and blinked a few times, hoping her vision would clear. But it didn't. Her view was blocked by....

She froze. It was Miles's chest she was looking at.

She was sleeping next to him. Not just sleeping next to him, either. They were turned in toward each other, her cheek up against his chest, her hand resting against his stomach, while one of his arms was draped over her and his chin sitting softly on the top of her head. She was small enough that she fit in the space like in a cocoon—warm, cozy, and meant for her.

Her heart hammered as she tried to remember how she had come to be in Miles's bed. No, it was her bed, not his. He had come in her room and taken Thomas from her. It had taken her a long time to fall asleep with Miles sitting on the other side of the bed, baby in his arms.

She frowned. She had a vague memory of pulling Miles toward her, and her cheeks warmed at the memory.

It was all hazy.

Gently, she moved herself away from Miles, sliding her head out from under his chin and pulling her hand from his body. The relative chill of the air made her skin prickle where it had been in contact with Miles. Part of her didn't want to move. But Thomas's fussing was growing louder.

She rolled out of bed and looked at Miles for a moment. He was so peaceful there. She had forgotten what he looked like when he slept, and her mouth curled up in a smile at the way his hair sat against his pillow. It would be a mess when he woke. It had always taken a great deal of water and pomade to tame it.

She hurried over to the cradle, avoiding all the spots on the floor she knew would creak, and picked up Thomas, swaying with him. His fussing quieted, and his eyes closed again. He just needed to be reassured.

She waited a moment before leaning over to set him back in his cradle, but the moment she set him down, he began writhing and fussing, and she was obliged to pick him up again.

Still Miles slept. Two more times, she rocked Thomas to sleep and tried to put him in the cradle, but he would have none of it. Her arms and back began to ache, and she looked at the place she had left in the bed with a twinge of longing. It was looking more enticing now, being held by Miles rather than holding Thomas—and for heaven only knew how long. She might well be rocking him for the rest of the night. They would both get more sleep if she simply took him in the bed with her.

She took Thomas with her to her side of the bed and, gaze on Miles, climbed back in with the baby in her arms. She lay down, letting Thomas rest in the crook of one arm.

Miles stirred, shifting and blinking. The corner of his mouth pulled up in a sleepy half-smile as his eyes settled upon her. Heart fluttering, she returned it.

"He insists upon being held," she said, looking down at Thomas.

Miles's blinks were slow, and he reached out a hand to set on the baby's head. "Let me take him." Even his words sounded half-asleep.

"No," she said. "He is content enough here that we can all sleep."

Miles's eyes closed, and he moved his head so that it rested against her arm, near to Thomas's head, and soon enough, sleep had overtaken both boys.

Lydia tried to suppress the emotion that rose in her throat. This was what she had always wanted. What *they* had always wanted. And while she knew it was but a temporary taste of heaven, tonight she would just accept it for what it was instead of anticipating when it would end.

She let her head rest on her pillow and pulled the coverlet over her.

"I love you," she said in a bare whisper. "Both of you." She allowed herself a few more seconds to admire them then shut her eyes and joined them in sleep.

❄

Lydia woke in the light of the morning to the sound of Thomas cooing musically beside her. Sometime during the night, she had pulled her arm from under him, and her hand cradled her cheek. One of her legs was tangled up with Miles's. She was conscious of mixed feelings of contentment and shyness at waking in her bed together, so much like old times.

She looked at him, and they caught eyes. His mouth was already drawn in a smile. He seemed to have been watching Thomas, supported by his elbow, head resting on the palm of his hand. His nightshirt hung down loosely, giving her an extensive view of his chest.

"He has been singing for a few minutes now," Miles said. "And attempting to eat his own feet."

"I cannot blame him," Lydia said, rising up on her elbow. "I am hungry too." The shoulder of her chemise fell, slipping halfway down her arm, and she hurried to pull it back up.

Miles's eyes followed the action then flitted quickly away. A bundle of nerves formed in her stomach. She loved the intimacy of sleeping in her bed with Miles, of being close. But the thought of *more* intimacy brought on a hint of desire quickly overwhelmed by fear.

She got out of bed and donned her wrapper then reached for Thomas, bringing him into her arms and letting him sit upright. He smiled at her, mouth open wide. He was irresistibly happy in the mornings.

"Good morning to you, too," she said. "Shall we find you something to eat?"

Jane arrived a few minutes later, and from her place in the doorway, her gaze shot over to Miles, who was sitting on the edge of the bed. Lydia felt another flutter of nerves and embarrassment. What sort of things did the servants say about them? And what did they think of Thomas? What would they say to know that Miles had slept in Lydia's room?

Lydia handed Thomas over to Jane. "Would you feed him? You can bring him to me in the breakfast room in…say, half an hour?"

Jane gave a small curtsy and left.

Lydia took her time shutting the door. She was alone with Miles now, and the prospect thrilled and paralyzed her. But she couldn't avoid him now. Or what had happened.

"Hopefully he will be happy today," she said, turning back toward him and making her way over to the bed. She occupied herself with straightening pillows—a silly task on a bed which would be made later by the maids.

"He seems cheerful enough so far," Miles said. "Perhaps he is not so sick after all." His hair stuck up on his right side, just as Lydia had anticipated it would, and she couldn't stop a smile.

He narrowed his eyes at her, though his mouth turned up at the side. "What is it?"

"Nothing," she said. "Only your hair…"

He put a hand up to feel his head and pushed the hair down hurriedly. "Dratted hair. *Every single morning.*"

"Yes," she laughed. "I remember. Here." She came over to him, and he searched her face before lowering his head so she could reach it. She paused a moment then raked both hands through his hair so that it all stood on end. He caught at her wrists, bringing his head back up, and she covered her laugh with a hand.

"*That* was not what I was expecting you to do," he said, trying to stifle his own smile. He still held her wrists. "And after I handled your hair with such gentleness last night?" He made a *tsk*ing sound then let one of her hands fall, touching a finger to her hair and holding her eyes with a teasing look that promised vengeance. But he only brushed the hair away from her face, letting his fingers comb through the strands all the way to the end, halfway down her arm.

Lydia suddenly felt lightheaded, and her gaze moved to Miles's lips, remembering how it had felt to kiss him under the kissing bough.

There, they had been watched. Here, they were all alone. Would it feel the same? She wanted to explore what she had felt, to know if there was any chance that they could recapture what they had once had.

He leaned in closer, his eyes searching her face then roving to her mouth.

But they had been down this road before. It led nowhere. She knew that. Did *he*? How could she expect him to resign himself to the fact that he had married a woman who couldn't do the one thing she was meant to do?

"I should get dressed," she said, pulling away slightly. "I told Jane to bring Thomas in half an hour."

Miles blinked then nodded. "Yes, yes. Of course. I should prepare for the day as well." He hesitated before giving a perfunctory smile and making his way toward the door to his room. When the door shut behind him, Lydia clenched her eyes shut.

❄

Thomas was certainly happier than he had been the day before, but Lydia was exhausted. By the time dinner was finishing, she couldn't stifle a yawn.

"You have yawned no fewer than four times since dinner began," Diana said. "Why don't you let Jane take the little foundling tonight? It would do you good to have a full night of rest. If he continues to feel out of sorts, you shall need all the sleep you can get. Besides, he seems to be well enough today."

"He does," Lydia said, but she balked at the idea of letting him sleep elsewhere. He had become a comfort to her in her room. Whenever she looked over at him in his cradle, she could almost imagine she was living the life she had dreamed of. But it was just that: a dream.

She couldn't deny she was exhausted, though, and the prospect of a night of undisturbed sleep was enticing. "I think you are right, though. Perhaps for tonight, we can move his cradle to Jane's room."

The four of them played a few games of whist after dinner was over, and Lydia caught Miles looking at her a number of times. What was he thinking? They used to talk so freely with one another. But things were different now. She had too many thoughts and feelings he wouldn't approve of. And certainly he must, too. It was those suspected thoughts which had plagued her for so long now.

When the final game concluded, they made their way upstairs together, and Diana and Mary bade them goodnight as Lydia and Miles stopped before his door again. Lydia swallowed nervously.

The door to Diana's and Mary's bedchambers closed, and Lydia glanced at her husband. There it was. That uncertain look in his eyes again. The one that made the guilt burgeon inside her, as if he was afraid she might strike him if he said anything.

"Would you like to come in?" he asked.

What was the answer to his question? She didn't know. All she knew was she was tired of rejecting him, tired of keeping her walls up, tired of sleeping alone. She was *tired*.

She swallowed and nodded, and the smile she was rewarded with gave her a bit of courage. He took her by the hand and led her into his room. She hardly knew what she was agreeing to by coming with him. Did he want to talk? To sleep beside her again? To finish the kiss they'd nearly had that morning. Or did he want...more?

He pulled her along until they came to the bed, and her heart beat wildly as he turned toward her.

"Lydia," he said, and he put a hand to her face.

His words, his hand—they were so gentle. They always were.

"Yes?"

He looked down into her eyes then rested his forehead against hers. "Last night, being beside you again....I haven't slept so well in months."

His nose brushed lightly against hers, and she shut her eyes as his hand went to her waist.

"It gave me hope," he said.

She stilled. "Hope?"

"Yes," he said. "It has been so long since..."

She drew back slightly, her stomach flooding with waves of nausea. She couldn't do this. Couldn't allow him to think that there *was* hope. It would crush her—the expectation, the disappointment. All over again. Month after month after month. She couldn't bear it. This was all a mistake.

She broke away. "I can't, Miles. There is no purpose to....I can't." She put the back of her hand to her mouth and hurried from the room.

CHAPTER 15

Miles stared at the door that shut softly behind Lydia. She hadn't even used the door to her bedchamber. She'd used the one to the corridor, as if, in her hurry to leave, she was also rejecting the little connection they had managed to develop over the past few days.

He ran a hand through his hair, and the gesture reminded him of the playful way Lydia had done just that this morning. What had happened to so suddenly drive her away? What was it she had said? *There is no purpose to...*And she had left it unfinished. No purpose to holding one another? To the hope he had mentioned?

He had been too quick, too eager to pull her into his arms. He hadn't intended to. He had wanted her company, more than anything. And perhaps to lay together as they had done the night before, but this time, he had wanted to be certain that it was what she wanted and not simply because she was too tired to know exactly what she was doing. And when she had agreed to come in with him, he had been so relieved and surprised, he had let his impulses take over. He wanted her to know how much he yearned for a reconciliation between them, to feel his love for her.

Miles slumped down on the bed and dropped his head in his hands, rubbing at his forehead harshly. He had scared her away. She didn't *want* any of that. Had she not made that abundantly clear over the past year? She no longer wished for that sort of relationship with him. What she wanted was a child, and Miles couldn't give her one.

Besides, she had Thomas now. What did she need Miles for?

❅

The next morning, Lydia didn't show any sign that she resented him for what had happened in his room the night before. She didn't mention it at all. She was, as usual, focused on Thomas, whose fussiness over the past two days was discovered to be due to the tooth that had popped through his bottom gums.

Lydia congratulated him on his achievement, and Miles had to stifle a scoff. As if Thomas had done anything personally to deserve praise for sprouting a tooth. He hardly could have prevented it.

Miles nipped such thoughts in the bud. Was he truly going to allow things with Lydia to sour how he felt about something like Thomas gaining a tooth?

He needed to get out of the house. It would be good for Lydia to have some time with her sisters without him there. They had been around each other more in the past week than they had been for many months before. Perhaps they both needed some time away. His mother had sent a message over with one of her servants that morning anyway. She seemed to be feeling neglected. He would pay her a visit.

"Oh," his mother said in blinking surprise when he stepped into the parlor. "I thought you would bring the others." She sat before a tray piled with biscuits.

He stooped to give her a kiss on the cheek. "You mustn't sound so disappointed, Mother."

"Come now. I could never be disappointed in a nice coze with my eldest. Do sit down and help me eat this mountain of biscuits."

Miles took a seat and gladly obliged. His mother always provided the most delectable biscuits.

"What are the Donnely sisters doing, then?" she asked. "Surely they haven't gone out in this weather."

"No," he replied. "They are at home. Playing with Thomas, I imagine, or perhaps sitting at the pianoforte."

His mother's brows went up. "The baby is still there, then."

"Yes."

"How long do you mean to keep him? Were you not looking for a situation?"

Miles shifted in his seat. "Well, you know how busy everyone is right now. We had intended to wait until everything settles down after Christmastide has come to an end—and the weather isn't quite so cold."

She put down her teacup with a pinching of the lips. She disapproved. He wasn't surprised, but he had never outgrown the discomfort he felt when he knew his mother was dissatisfied with his decisions. Her approval was so rarely given that he found himself craving the way it felt to have it. It had been quite some time since he had received it.

"I hardly see what the weather has to do with it."

He shrugged. "There are more people in need when it's as cold as it is now. I imagine we will have more luck finding a good situation in a week or so."

"That may be, but at what cost to yourselves?"

He frowned and took another biscuit. "What do you mean?"

"My dear, does it not concern you how"—she hesitated—"well, how obsessed Lydia is with the child?"

Miles swallowed. "Not obsessed, surely."

She shot him a significant look. "She insists on feeding it, putting it to sleep, keeping it with her when company is there—things most women don't even do for their own children."

Miles didn't miss the way she referred to Thomas as *it* rather than *he*. "It is her personality to be so caring. You know that."

She gave a reluctant nod. "I don't say it to criticize her. Only that it worries me. For her sake and for yours."

"Why?"

She tipped her head from side to side as though debating, but Miles had the sense that what she was about to say had been on her mind for some time. "She is getting no younger, you know, and time is of the essence. The last thing she needs is something to distract her from the task before her. You *need* an heir, my dear. And, sweet as he might be, that little baby is not your heir."

Miles suppressed the urge to pull on his cravat, which was feeling too snug. It wasn't as though he had forgotten that he needed an heir—indeed, how could he?—but such an aggressive reminder of the fact, and from his mother specifically....It brought on the feelings of ineptitude and failure he had managed to evade over the past week or so.

She was looking at him thoughtfully, but she dropped her gaze to her teacup, running a finger along the tip. "Everything is well with you two, I take it?"

His brows drew together.

She cleared her throat. "I mean to say, nothing is amiss in your...*relations*?"

Miles's eyes widened, and he felt a rush of heat rise up his neck and into his cheeks. "Mother, I..."

She hurriedly set her teacup down. "I don't mean to pry. Only, I have known cases where women are disinclined to raise children and yet have convinced their husbands otherwise. Taking pennyroyal or ergot in secret to prevent pregnancy."

He clenched his jaw together, fighting off the anger and frustration he felt at the implication that Lydia was concealing something like that from him. "I can think of no woman who wants a child more than Lydia does."

"I've upset you," she said with apology in her eyes. "I assure you, I didn't intend to. I just...I so want you to be happy, my dear. I would never wish for you to be deprived of the very great joy I—or your father—have felt as your parents. Your success is my only aim in even mentioning such a delicate topic. I hope you know that."

He let out a breath through his nose and offered an apologetic smile. "Of course, Mother. I could never doubt it."

She reached for his hand and pressed it within hers. "You are meant for great things, Miles. I have always known it."

CHAPTER 16

Lydia watched Miles with a bit of apprehension on his return from his mother's. As foolish as it was, she could never keep herself from fearing that, anytime he was with his mother outside of Lydia's company, the dowager baroness was doing work to turn Miles against her. It was an unreasonable thing to think, and yet the suspicion crept in despite her best efforts.

He *did* seem to be a bit more withdrawn, and his greeting of Thomas was more disinterested than usual. She felt guilt and regret creep into her. Had her rejection last night sent him back into his shell? She couldn't blame him, really. She was impossible to please. Too much affection shown on his part, and she ran away; not enough, and she felt neglected, unwanted. But how did she stop feeling that way? She could pretend, she could act, but what good would that do?

Miles spent the better part of the afternoon in the study, conducting some matters of business he claimed he had been putting off, while Lydia and her sisters delved into a book Lydia had found at the lending library before the cold had set in. She laughed along with Diana and Mary, but the truth was, she felt anxious inside. She had tasted what it felt to be back in Miles's arms, and she was terrified that she would ruin any future chance of it happening again—that perhaps she already had.

"Is Jane prepared to take care of Thomas tomorrow evening?" Miles asked as they sat at dinner.

Lydia gave him a questioning look. "I...I didn't know she would need to."

He paused with his hand over his soup, looking at her. "It is the Gallaghers' dinner party."

"Oh," she said. "I had entirely forgotten."

"I'm afraid I already sent our acceptance more than a week ago. I don't feel like I can forgo it after Gallagher's support of the bill I'm putting forward when Parliament begins again. There *will* be dancing."

She didn't want to go, in truth. She had used to enjoy such gatherings, but they had lost much of their pleasure over the years. She inevitably returned home feeling like a failure after hearing their friends and acquaintances talk of their burgeoning families and being urged and asked about when they might expect to see Lydia's and Miles's family grow.

"Do you wish for me to go alone? Make your excuses?" It was asked without any accusation, but Lydia didn't miss the guarded look that came into Miles's eyes. He was already expecting her refusal.

"No," she said with a smile. "I will go with you, of course. Thomas will be asleep by then, anyway. And Jane is capable of ensuring he has everything he needs if he *does* wake."

Miles smiled at her, the bit of strain in his eyes disappearing. He was pleased with her response. And she would do her best to ensure he had an enjoyable evening. This was a chance to reconnect, and she couldn't waste it.

❄

For the first time in recent memory, Lydia took great pains with her toilette, giving much more instruction to Sarah than was her custom. She ran a nervous, gloved hand down her dress, a red satin that looked rose-colored with its embroidered gauze overlay. She wanted to be a credit to Miles—as much as she could be, at least.

When she joined him in the entry hall, the look of admiration in his eyes and the way he brought her hand to his lips sent a little thrill up her spine. It was reassurance enough that she had done right to join him. They needed each other, didn't they?

He handed her up into the carriage and hesitated for the briefest of seconds before sitting beside her rather than across from her. He spread a fur rug across her legs then hit a fist on the roof, and the carriage pulled forward.

"Thank you," he said, and he took her hand in his. "For coming, I mean. I know it isn't easy for you to leave Thomas."

She looked over at him, searching his eyes as much as the dim light of the carriage would allow. What did he think of her attachment to Thomas? "Am I silly to worry over him?"

He stared at her for a moment then shook his head, but he said nothing, and both of them were left with their thoughts for the short journey to the Gallaghers'.

The street was lined with carriages, with men helping ladies out of the carriage and onto the icy streets. It was a larger party than Lydia had anticipated, and the knowledge made her feel nervous all over again.

"Good evening, Lord and Lady Lynham," said Mrs. Gallagher as they entered. "How wonderful to see you. I'm afraid my husband is speaking over there with Lord Napley, but I'm sure he will find you at some point this evening. We weren't entirely certain who we could expect. There are many more people in Town than is generally the case at this time of year, but so many are keeping indoors. I should have known I could depend on you."

"We wouldn't have missed it," Miles said.

Mrs. Gallagher squeezed Lydia's hand. "*You* are certainly looking lovely this evening, Lady Lynham. You have always been a great beauty—I forget just how lovely until I see you. If I'm not mistaken, I recognize the glow you have about you." She smiled conspiratorially.

Lydia's own smile faltered, and she tried to reinforce it. The attempt fell woefully flat, she knew.

"Thank you for inviting us, Mrs. Gallagher," Miles said. "We are always happy for an opportunity to see you."

She wished them an enjoyable evening and turned to the next guests.

Miles covered the hand Lydia had on his arm with his own, pressing it lightly in a comforting gesture. "She is right, you know. You *are* looking lovely this evening."

She gave him a grateful look. Mrs. Gallagher would be mortified if she discovered her offhand compliment had elicited such discomfort from Lydia. But that was just it. No one *tried* to make her feel badly about their lack of children. Everyone intended well. But they couldn't possibly fathom the ache their words brought to her heart or the burden that hundreds of such conversations could amount to over time.

Would there ever be a time when people simply realized that Lord and Lady Lynham would never have children of their own? The weight of everyone's hope was nearly as crushing as the weight of Lydia's despair. If only people could resign themselves to the fact, she might be able to begin doing so as well. And Miles, too. But of course their words must always be reminding him of what he didn't have.

She took in a fortifying breath and let her eyes rove over the crowds.

"Would you like to dance?" Miles asked.

"Yes," she said. "Please." Dancing had a way of reviving her spirits and distracting her in just the way she needed. It was a country dance forming on the ballroom floor, and Lydia felt her mood lifting as soon as she stepped into place in the set. The way Miles smiled at her from across set her heart aflutter and made her forget Mrs. Gallagher's words.

They had been to many balls together in the past year, but dancing had been rare, generally only done when they had been pressured to do so by an acquaintance. It had been polite and formulaic. Tonight, though, was different. Miles's gaze stayed trained on her the entire time, and the usual mistakes he made had Lydia laughing and her cheeks sore by the end of the set.

Some couples remained, while others broke from the line to seek refreshment. Miles offered up his arm to Lydia, and they followed the latter parties.

"Lord Lynham!"

Lydia glanced over, and the smile on her lips faltered. It was Lord and Lady Venton, leaving the dance floor as well. How had she not noticed that they had been among the set? Or at the party at all? She couldn't resist a look at Miles, and he looked just as surprised as she did.

"Lord Venton," he said, inclining his head. "Lady Venton."

She smiled at both of them, and Lydia felt a bit nauseated. Lydia had wondered if she had perhaps idealized Lady Venton in her mind, but no. She had decidedly not.

"I say, Lady Lynham," Lord Venton said. "Will you not dance with me? My wife says she is too tired for another set, but I know you can always be relied upon to join a man on the ballroom floor."

"Oh," Lydia said. She had never danced with the man, but she hardly felt she could refuse him after such words. "I would be glad to do so."

"Splendid," he said, handing off his wife to Miles. "Lynham, perhaps you can take Sophia to the refreshment table. She is always wishing for a morsel these days. Perhaps you heard—she is in the family way again."

Lydia's stomach flooded with more nausea.

"My mother had mentioned that," Miles said, losing none of his genial way. Lydia wished she had his same measure of composure. "I congratulate you both on such a happy announcement."

"The two of you better get going," Lord Venton said with a wink at Lydia and Miles, "if you intend to catch up with us."

Lord Venton was an amiable gentleman—handsome and easy to converse with—and Lydia tried her best to keep her attention on him during the set. She was successful for almost the entirety of the first dance, but then the dance took Lord Venton away for a moment, leaving her to stand in line with nothing to keep her attention. Her eyes sought Miles, and they found him with no trouble at all.

Her stomach clenched. He was still with Lady Venton. They were laughing, with a drink in hand, and they were beautiful together. Looking at them there—Lady Venton with her rounding stomach, Miles looking particularly handsome in his breeches—it was almost like looking at a picture of an alternate reality. It was everything Miles *could* have had if he had never met Lydia—if he had listened to his mother and father and done what he had planned to do.

An arm scooped around Lydia's, and she blinked and scurried back into the dance, grateful that Lord Venton was amusing himself far too well to note the embarrassing tears in her eyes.

CHAPTER 17

SEPTEMBER 1810

Miles hated to see his father this way—the raspy breathing, the sunken cheeks, the hacking coughs that made Miles clench his fists for fear his father might never manage to catch his breath again.

He was on the edge of his seat, a glass of water at the ready, but his father waved it away as he finally managed to stop coughing, dropping back onto the pillows behind him and looking more tired and drawn than ever.

"Help me lie down," he said, and Miles set down the glass of water, hurrying up to help his father shift down farther in the bed. "It is time, Miles," he said.

Miles swallowed. He wasn't ready for this. Was one ever ready to say goodbye to a parent?

"It is time for you and Lydia to get serious about an heir," his father continued, eyes still closed. "It is unwise to put it off."

Miles blinked in surprise and debated for a moment how to respond. It wasn't as though he and Lydia had been avoiding having a child. But perhaps they did need to pursue things more seriously now, whatever that meant.

"I had hoped the succession might be secure by the time I died. But..." His father's brow furrowed. "Promise me you won't delay any longer."

"I promise, Father," Miles said with a lump in his throat. His children would never meet their grandfather.

"I have no doubt you and he will make me proud," his father said. "The seventh and eighth Barons Lynham. An unbroken succession." He breathed through the hint of a smile, as though the prospect brought him a sense of peace.

❄

The Present

Miles hoped the smile he wore hid his impatience as he glanced at the ballroom floor. Venton had asked Lydia to join him for the two longest dances of the night.

It wasn't that he minded keeping Sophia company. They had always gotten along very well—he would never have considered marrying her if it weren't for that fact. Nor did he begrudge her the joy of a life that seemed to hit every milestone and success with the clockwork precision of the Mail Coach.

He merely envied her situation and her achievements. He wanted the same for him and Lydia.

He looked to Lydia again. She had perhaps never looked so beautiful as she did now, but there was something amiss, something about her smile that wasn't entirely genuine. If only he could be the one to fix that. But nothing he did seemed to help—at least not for more than a moment. Whenever he thought they were turning a corner, it turned out not to be so, and she retreated from him again. He feared that, at some point, she might do so for good.

"Have you and Lady Lynham been passing an agreeable

Christmastide?" Sophia asked. "Despite this terrible cold, I mean. It has certainly forced a great many people to change their plans. I had understood that you intended to spend Christmas in Staffordshire."

He nodded. "The best laid plans, you know. But we have managed to keep ourselves entertained here in Town, all the same. My wife's sisters joined us, and they are...well, let us just say that they entertain us well enough themselves."

Sophia's mouth pulled into a smile. "If they are anything like Lady Lynham, I can only imagine they have brightened the season immeasurably."

The set finally finished, but Lydia was stopped by a friend on her way over, so Venton came alone to retrieve his wife. He thanked Miles for taking her into his care, and the two of them retreated to a different part of the room.

A hand clapped upon Miles's shoulder, and he turned, stifling a sigh as he encountered George Hewitt and Edward Parry, friends of Harry. Hewitt was a tiresome companion for conversation. He imagined himself to be quite entertaining, but the truth was, he was simply annoying. And as for Parry, he was certainly preferable to Hewitt, but only marginally so. Why Harry insisted upon keeping such company, Miles couldn't understand. He tried to be kind to them for his brother's sake, but the men were both fools.

"What has you wearing such a Friday face, Lynham?" Hewitt asked, squeezing Miles's shoulder and shaking it slightly.

"Surely not a Friday face." Miles removed Hewitt's hand and made an effort to look more pleasant. He was normally better at hiding what he was feeling.

"An undeniable Friday face," Hewitt replied. "Here." He took the empty glass from Miles's hand and set it on the tray of the passing footman, who paused so Hewitt could take three new ones. He gave one to Miles and one to Parry.

"What's this we hear of a little baby in your house?" Parry asked.

Miles felt a renewed desire to throttle his brother. Why must he insist upon spreading the news about to people like Hewitt and Parry? If they knew, it was likely that all of London did.

He shrugged, hoping his nonchalance would convince them that it was a matter of too little importance to dwell upon. "We found him at the Frost Fair and couldn't leave him there in good conscience. He seems to have been abandoned by his mother."

"Ah. Much better than what I had heard."

Miles turned to look at him, but Hewitt was gazing around the ballroom. He winked at someone.

"And what, may I ask, did you hear?" Miles said.

Hewitt tossed off his glass. "Thought you were perhaps hoping to pass him off as your own." He winked at Miles, and Parry chuckled.

"What a feat that would be!" Parry cried out. "A stranger's brat in line for the Barony of Lynham!" He slapped a hand on his thigh in amusement. "I wish you *would*, Lynham! It would be great sport to watch you dupe the *ton* with such a trick."

"Best your father isn't here to see such a thing, eh?" Hewitt said with a jab of the elbow in Miles's side. "He would not have been amused in the least, would he?"

"Hardly," Miles said, hoping to quell any cause the two men might have to believe Miles wished for further discussion on the subject.

Parry tilted his head from side to side, as though considering this. "No, I suppose not. And we wouldn't want to serve Harry such a trick, either. Not when he's got a chance at the title!"

"Very true," Hewitt responded.

Miles felt his pulse in his neck. Most of the time, their banter was harmless, but tonight it had a barb to it Miles didn't want to admit.

"Saw you talking to Lady Venton," Parry said, gesturing in her direction with his glass.

"Your powers of observation are formidable, Parry," Miles said sardonically.

"Thank you," Parry said, missing the insult. "Now *there's* a couple who will have more children than they know what to do with if they keep on as they are."

Hewitt chuckled. "It's like Jacobs used to say about him and his wife—they need only look at one another to have her with child yet again! Six of 'em already, though four of 'em are girls, you know." He shook his head as though this was cause for lament. "Perhaps they'd lend you one of the boys, Lynham. I imagine they'll have a few more by the time they're done."

Miles balled his fists and smiled through clenched teeth. "And perhaps they'll lend a daughter to each of you, since I have grave doubts either of you will be able to find a woman who will have you without an added dose of persuasion. Good evening, gentlemen."

He walked toward the French doors that led out onto the terrace. They were closed—it was far too cold outside to leave them open—but Miles needed some air, and he pulled a handle and slipped outside.

He sucked in a long breath, focusing on how the frigid air felt traveling down his throat and into his lungs. It was silly of him to let Hewitt's and Parry's mindless jabbering bother him. Why should it matter to him what anyone thought of him or Lydia? Or Thomas, for that matter? It was none of their business.

But it *did* matter to him. And hearing the Lynham succession discussed as though Harry were the heir apparent rather than the heir presumptive? It was evidence of how people saw Miles as a failure.

And the things that were undoubtedly being said about them taking in a baby...

He clenched his eyes shut against the way his pride smarted and thought of the letter he'd received earlier that day from his mother. She'd informed him she had found a situation for Thomas.

He hadn't told Lydia. He wasn't sure how to. He could already foresee the dismay in her eyes.

The door creaked open, and he turned to see Lydia herself come outside. She shivered, pulling her long gloves up to cover the gap between them and her sleeves.

"What are you doing out here, Miles? It is frigid." She searched his face and slowed. "What is it?"

"Nothing," he said, shaking his head. He wouldn't trouble her with the gossip. "Shall we leave? I find I have had my fill of the company here."

She smiled at him and nodded. "I should like that."

CHAPTER 18

They made their way back through the crowds inside, Miles pulling Lydia along, obviously impatient to leave. To those who greeted him, he offered a nod and a smile. Normally, he would stop and spend a minute or two greeting them, but not tonight.

Lydia swallowed, glancing at Lady Venton one last time. Was it his conversation with her which had made him wish to leave? Was it too painful to be in her presence, knowing what he could have had but had foregone?

Lydia let out a large sigh as they settled into the carriage seat together.

"Quite so," Miles said.

She didn't respond, too unsure what his mood meant to know what might aggravate it. The only sound was of coachmen calling to each other as the carriage carefully navigated away from the Gallaghers' townhouse, followed by carriage wheels rumbling and horse hooves clacking on the cobbled streets.

"Tomorrow marks the beginning of a new year," Miles said after a minute or two of silence.

"It does, doesn't it?" Usually she looked forward to the prospect of a fresh year, but all she could feel was anxiousness at the thought of what 1815 might bring. She had lost her confidence in the future.

"Before we know it, it will be Epiphany."

She looked at him, trying to understand why he would mention that day specifically. He was watching her, too.

"We agreed we would try to find a situation for Thomas by Twelfth Night," he said, "and I haven't made a single inquiry into the matter, I'm afraid."

Her muscles tensed. "Well, we didn't necessarily set the date in stone. We merely said that we should likely be able to find something by then."

He narrowed his eyes at her, as though he was trying to see through her words. "We cannot put it off indefinitely."

She paused before responding. It had been silly to hope that things might turn out just that way—an intention that never materialized. But she realized now that she *had* hoped it. Deep down, she had been hoping that Miles was getting just as attached to Thomas as she was, that he wouldn't wish to part with him at all, that he would forget about finding him another home entirely.

"No, I suppose not," she said with a catch in her throat.

Of course it wasn't what he wished. He didn't just want a baby. He wanted an *heir*. And, no matter how much he cared for Thomas and wanted the best for him, Thomas could never be his heir.

❈

It was a lonely end to a lonely year, and instead of letting Thomas sleep in his cradle, Lydia brought him in bed with her, to sleep where he and Miles had slept just three nights ago.

How would she bear the solitude when Thomas left? She pushed down the emotion in her throat as she gazed at his long, curled lashes.

"I wish you could stay," she said in a whisper, and her breath ruffled a few of the fine hairs that peeked out from the cap on his head.

The dowager baroness had promised to join them for tea the next afternoon, and when Lydia heard her mother-in-law's voice coming from downstairs, she cringed. She had hoped that she and the dowager baroness would manage to get along more easily, but instead, it was getting more difficult as time went on.

"And how was the Gallaghers' party last night?" she asked of Miles as Lydia poured the tea. Mary and Diana had declined to join them, and Lydia envied them.

She hardly knew how to respond to the dowager's question, so she was grateful when Miles stepped in. "It was...more crowded than I had expected. We did not stay long."

The dowager looked at Lydia, indicating her arms with a nod. "How strange to see you without that baby in your arms. Did you find a place for him, then?"

Lydia felt her heart begin to patter more quickly. "No. I asked Jane to put him down to sleep before I came down."

"I see." She smiled in a way Lydia found patronizing, almost as if she pitied her. "Well, I am sure Miles told you I may have discovered a situation for little Thomas."

Lydia glanced at Miles, who was looking down at his hands, a frown on his face. Would he step in and tell her that they didn't need her to take the task upon herself?

"I am waiting to receive word back," she continued. "But I am hopeful that it will serve, and I will, of course, inform you as soon as I know."

Miles seemed to be avoiding Lydia's eye, and it was all she could do to thank her mother-in-law and change the subject as quickly as possible.

When it came time to see the dowager baroness out, Lydia and Miles accompanied her to the door. Lydia waited for it to shut behind her mother-in-law then turned without a look at Miles and made her way up the stairs.

"Lydia," he said, following behind her.

She turned toward him once she reached the top of the stairs, trying to breathe evenly. Her patience had worn thin after an hour with the dowager baroness, and she found that her chest was rising and falling quickly. She was frustrated with Miles—with his silence. With the fact that he had told her nothing of his mother's meddling despite their conversation the night before about finding Thomas a home.

He checked on the final stair, searching her face. "You are angry."

She said nothing in response. It wasn't a question anyway. It was a statement. And it was true.

"Is it because my mother has found a place for Thomas?"

"When you told her we did not require her assistance in the matter?" Lydia asked. "Yes, that is part of it."

"But only part of it..." he said slowly, searching her face.

"Once again, you allow her to—" she stopped, letting out a breath through her nose and looking away. "We have already discussed this. There is little purpose to doing so again."

He made an incredulous sound, but she was tired of feeling like she had to beg him to stand up for them to his mother. He had said it before: he didn't care to cross his mother. He would rather allow her free rein to avoid hurting her feelings or confronting her, even if it meant causing Lydia pain.

"You said nothing when she mentioned the situation for Thomas," Lydia said. "I take it that means you wish for it?"

"I take it you don't?"

She swallowed, and he stared at her.

"You want to keep him, don't you?" he asked.

Her nostrils flared, and her eyes burned. "And you want to be rid of him as soon as possible, don't you?"

He put his hands up, as though trying to defend himself from an attacking animal. "I have nothing but Thomas's best interests at heart. You *know* I care for him."

"But?"

His jaw shifted from side to side. "Do you know what they are saying about him? About us?"

"Who?"

He threw up his hands. "The Town."

She felt a sickness settle in the pit of her stomach. She hated knowing that people discussed them. "I'm sure it makes no difference to me what people choose to say or believe about any of it."

"Then you are better than I, for I *do* care. I wish I didn't." He set a hand on his hips and rubbed the other across his lips.

"What do their opinions matter, Miles? Is Thomas not more important than the gossip of people so bored by their own lives they insist upon discussing the lives of others? Do you not feel how utterly fatuous hearsay is when compared with more weighty matters, like the well-being of an innocent child?"

He shut his eyes and shook his head from side to side. "It is not so easy or simple as that, Lydia. As I said, I want the best for Thomas. I truly do. But it is like a stab in the heart every time I see you fawning over the child of a stranger when you seem to have given up hope on having one of our own. And then to face the humiliation of going amongst friends, as we did last night..."

She clenched her hands to counteract the pang in her heart. "You say friends, but that is not what you mean, is it?"

His brows contracted. "What?"

"I can only think your humiliation and the reason you wished to leave so quickly last night was because of the time you spent with *her*."

His frown deepened. "Her? You mean Lady Venton?"

Lydia swallowed. "The woman you wish you had married. I am sure it is humiliating to you to be seen by her. With your barren wife." She stopped before her voice could break and betray her. "Perhaps you are right, though, to wish to rid yourself of Thomas. How can we bring a child into *this*?" She motioned at the space between them. "We barely ever talk. How could we possibly raise a child together?"

She hurried into her room before her emotions could overtake her.

CHAPTER 19

Miles walked dazedly to his room, standing inside the shut door for some time, stunned, trying to determine just what precisely he was feeling.

He was frustrated at her insistence that there was no purpose in discussing things together. She had used the same words when he had invited her into his room just two nights ago. *No purpose.* How was anything to change between them if she thought there was no purpose to talking, no purpose to being near one another?

But foremost in his mind was her reference to Lady Venton. *The woman you wish you had married*, she had said. Is that what she truly thought?

Had he given her reason to? He never spoke of Sophia, and for good reason. He never even thought of her except when he happened to see her at the odd party or gathering. But, even then, he certainly didn't wish he had married her. He merely envied her—he wanted to see Lydia as content with life as Sophia seemed to be. That was all.

He rubbed his temples with his fingers, letting out a great sigh. Lydia needed to know she was wrong, and she needed to hear it from his lips.

Hand shaking slightly as he approached the door connecting their bedchambers, he rapped softly. Would she even answer?

The door opened, and Miles could see evidence of tears wiped hastily away. The sight of it ached in his chest. Had he made her so miserable? It was all he had been doing for a long time, it seemed.

"Lydia," he said softly, putting out a hand toward her cheek.

She pulled back slightly, and her throat bobbed as her eyes filled even more.

He dropped his hand. "Would you come in?" The wariness in her eyes was evident immediately, and he tried not to focus on his own hurt. "I just want to talk," he said.

She hesitated for a moment then passed through, turning toward him once he had shut the door.

"Lydia, I..." He pressed his lips together, unsure how to communicate what needed saying. They were so very out of practice, so unused to expressing emotion to one another. But he could feel his marriage falling apart, and he had to rise above his hesitation to be vulnerable if he stood any chance of saving it.

She had her arms folded, not in a challenging way but almost as though she was trying to comfort herself—protect herself.

"When we chose to marry," he said, "I was determined that you should never regret your decision. I would lavish you with love, see to your every need, give you no reason to complain of me as a husband. As a father to your children." He swallowed down the emotion determinedly and looked at his hands, clasped in front of him. "I have failed in every regard."

There was silence, the only sound breaking it a sniffle.

"But I would have you know that it is not for lack of love of you, Lydia." He looked up at her. "I have never once regretted marrying you. Nor have I ever wished myself married to Lady Venton. You *must* believe that."

She shut her eyes, and more tears squeezed onto her cheeks.

He stepped toward her then checked. He had promised her he only wished to talk, and he wouldn't give her reason to think he had said such a thing to manipulate her into coming in. "If I have given you reason to believe such a lie, I don't know how I shall forgive myself." He balled his hands into fists to keep himself in place. "Tell me you believe me, Lydia. Tell me I haven't been such a terrible husband that you believe my heart is anywhere but with you."

A little sob escaped her, and she hurried toward him, wrapping her arms about him.

Stunned, he received her gladly then shut his eyes, pressing a kiss upon the top of her head as he held her close. "Tell me I haven't lost you."

She said nothing, but her head shook from side to side against his chest, her arms pulling him toward her as if to echo her unsaid words.

They stood there, holding one another, Miles stroking her hair, for what seemed like an eternity. Still not long enough to make up for all the time they had lost.

Finally, she pulled her head away, looking up at him, eyes still shining with the remnants of her tears. But there was a hint of hope and joy in them now.

She went up on her tiptoes, and Miles met her lips with his softly. He didn't want to overwhelm her, even though he wanted nothing more than to take her in his arms and remove any doubt whatsoever about how he felt for her. Their lips settled against each other, brushing softly so that Miles's lips tingled. She pulled back a bit, and Miles opened his eyes to look at her, to see whether she was already regretting the kiss.

But her eyes were closed, as if she was savoring it. She opened them slowly, and her gaze searched his before she wrapped an arm around his neck and pulled his lips down to hers, every bit as insistent and demanding as the previous kiss had been timid and soft. Her hand moved from his neck, down to the lapels of his coat, tugging on them for a moment to bring him closer then pulling them to the side as if to remove them.

Miles hurried to help her, peeling the coat away from his shoulders and down his arms, mouth still locked on hers.

The coat fell to the ground, and he pulled back, catching his breath. He couldn't let himself be carried away, much as he might wish to—not if it jeopardized the future.

He stepped backward, needing the clarity the distance afforded. "Lydia. I don't wish for you to...to feel...pressured."

Her cheeks and lips were flushed with color, and she took a step toward him. "I want this."

He searched her face then nodded slowly, and she took another step toward him.

❋

Miles stirred and felt a kiss pressed to his brow. He frowned and opened his eyes slowly, his vision filling with the face of his wife, looking down at him.

She smiled with a hint of shyness in the fluttering of her lids, and he reached a hand up to her chin, pulling her toward him for a kiss.

"How long have you been awake?" he asked, glancing at the light coming through the curtains. It landed in glinting rays on the remnants of the dinnerware they had asked to be brought up the night before. Diana and Mary must have dined alone downstairs.

"Just a few minutes," Lydia replied. "I thought I heard Thomas crying, but I didn't want to leave you just yet."

He smiled widely then stilled, cocking an ear. "Yes, that's certainly him. What I wouldn't give for lungs like his."

Lydia pulled the sheet with her as she rolled to the other side of the bed. "I don't want Jane to go to my room, for she shan't find me there."

Miles reached for her hand, pulling her back onto the bed. "No, she certainly shan't. Not if I have anything to say to it, at least."

Lydia laughed and allowed him to bring her toward him.

"Jane can feed him, can she not?" he said between kisses.

She pulled away again, reaching for something on the floor and stepping into her chemise. "Thomas is getting more particular about who feeds him, I'm afraid. He seems to prefer I do it in the mornings." She bundled her other clothing in her arms and looked at him. "I can bring him in here if you'd like."

Miles smiled and nodded, and Lydia hurried to the door that led to her room.

When the door had shut, Miles lay back on his pillow with a sigh. He could have stayed there all morning alone with her. Indefinitely, really.

A few minutes later, Lydia returned, Thomas sitting in one arm, the bottle held precariously in the other hand. Miles gestured for her to relieve herself of one of her burdens, and she allowed him to take the bottle.

He scooted over in the bed, making room for her to sit beside him, and together they fed Thomas. The baby was in a particularly talkative mood once he had finished with his bottle, and he sat up on the bed, pulling the covers and anything within his reach to his mouth.

"You cannot eat that, my dear," Lydia said, her hand hovering behind his back to stabilize him. "I should have thought to bring your rattle. He favors it above any other toy he's been offered."

"I can get it," Miles said. "Where is it?"

Lydia pulled the covers away from Thomas yet again, grinning at him. "I cannot remember precisely. I may have put it on the desk in my room."

Miles quickly pulled on his shirt and trousers and hurried to her room, going straight to her desk. There was no rattle there. Only the usual inkpot and quill stand.

He pulled out the large drawer, and a glass bottle rolled toward him. A whiff of mint rushed by, and he pushed the bottle to the side, but his gaze caught on the word on its label. *Pennyroyal*.

He paused, staring at the word, trying to remember how he knew it. He picked up the bottle and turned it in his hands, uncorking the lid, which released another draught of the mint scent.

He froze. Pennyroyal. He remembered now. It was his mother who had mentioned it to him. A way to prevent pregnancy.

His breath started to come more quickly as he stared blankly at the word. He had dismissed his mother's words at the time. What had he said in response? Something about Lydia wanting a child more than anyone he knew.

He swallowed. Had he been wrong? Had it been an act? A way to pull the wool over his eyes about her true feelings, her true wishes?

His stomach roiled at the thought, and he set down the vial hurriedly, as though it was toxic. And apparently it *was*. Was this bottle the true reason they had not been able to conceive? The nausea built in his stomach, trying to travel up to his throat, and he forced it down with a painful swallow.

There had to be another reason.

The rattle was not in the drawer. Only the pennyroyal and a letter, which his eyes locked on. He didn't recognize the script Lydia's name was written in, and he only hesitated for a moment before taking the letter from the drawer. Perhaps it would explain the pennyroyal. Anything to help him understand why she had such a thing in her possession.

He unfolded the letter, letting his gaze first travel to the signature at the bottom.

James Coates
Coates & Lamming, Solicitors

Miles knew them by name, but that was all. Why would they be corresponding with Lydia?

His eyes ran as fast as they could over the contents of the letter, pressure building in his chest as he held his breath. The words cut at his heart like a scythe at dry crops.

He was vaguely aware of the sound of approaching footsteps.

"Miles? Is it not there? I am wondering if perhaps Jane didn't—" Lydia stopped on the threshold of her room, Thomas in her arms, eyes darting to the paper Miles held.

CHAPTER 20

The hurt in Miles's eyes was so at odds with the warm contentment she had seen in them just a few minutes ago that Lydia could do nothing but stand in place for a moment. She knew what letter he had in hand, though, and it was evident he had read it already.

Thomas grabbed her cheek with a frustrated gripe, and Miles's expression hardened, the hurt being replaced by a steely glint.

"Miles," she said, holding down Thomas's hand to keep him from repeating his gesture. "It was for your sake that I inquired."

He folded up the letter and set it back in the drawer, tucking it under the edge of the bottle of pennyroyal slowly and methodically. When he spoke, his voice was quiet but hard. "You accuse me of regretting our marriage, and yet I find you have been inquiring with a solicitor about how to obtain a divorce—or an annulment?"

She shook her head, walking over to him quickly. "Not because *I* wanted one," she said. "Only because I thought *you* did. Because I thought you deserved better than I could give you—than I *have* given you."

He glanced down again, his jaw shifting as he took up the vial of pennyroyal in his hand. "And this? Is this not the reason you have been unable to give me what you say I deserve? I can only assume you refer to an heir."

She blinked in confusion. "What?"

He swallowed—the first evidence that he was feeling any emotion but anger. "Have you been preventing pregnancy with this? And then inquiring with the solicitor whether a divorce could be obtained if no offspring had resulted from our marriage?"

It took her a moment to understand what he was accusing her of. "Miles, I—"

"How disappointing it must have been to discover that such a thing was not grounds for divorce or annulment after all." He set the vial on the desk with a clank.

Lydia's surprise began to transform to hurt—and anger to match his.

"You make a great number of assumptions about me," she said.

"Perhaps I do. But how am I to do anything else when you have avoided me for nigh on a year now?" He flicked the letter with a finger, and it slid farther across the desk, coming near to the edge. "What, then? Did you take Mr. Coates' advice into consideration? He made it quite clear that adultery was the only way out of a marriage like ours. Did you pursue *that* route when it became apparent that the pennyroyal was not enough to grant you a divorce?"

Her face screwed up, and she took a step back. "How dare you?" Thomas whined in her arms.

There was only the slightest flicker of hesitation in his face at her words. She had never seen him look so hard and cold.

"How dare I?" he asked. "You have obviously been keeping a number of secrets. How am I to know just what sort and how many? I deserve to know, do I not, whether my wife has been unfaithful?"

It took her a moment to respond, so close were her emotions to overwhelming her, to boiling over. "I have never even *thought* of another man in that way, and the fact that you would ask me such a question tells me that you know me not at all." Thomas began to cry, and she rocked him, though her rough movements betrayed her anger. "Thomas is crying. I must go."

"Oh, yes," he said. "Of course you must, for what is there in this world but Thomas?"

She stared at Miles for a moment then turned away.

"If we are discussing letters today," Miles said louder, "then I should perhaps inform *you* that my mother wrote to me. She received confirmation that Thomas will indeed be taken in by the family she found."

Lydia checked, swallowing convulsively and looking at the red, unhappy face of the baby in her arms. She looked back at Miles, but she could find no words to respond to him and turned to leave the room. But she stopped at the door again, pausing with her hand upon it. "In the unlikely case you care to hear the truth rather than assuming the worst of me, the pennyroyal is meant to bring back my courses, as I haven't had them in months now."

She pulled the door open and stepped into the corridor, shutting the door with a slam that immediately triggered a sob from somewhere deep inside her. It was hidden by the loudening cries of Thomas, whose bottom lip pouted and quivered in an expression that tore at her heart. He was scared. He may not have understood what was being said, but no doubt he had sensed the tension.

"There, there, my love," she said, resting her face against his and forcing a deep breath that trembled as it filled her lungs. "I am sorry for yelling. I'm not angry with *you*. Of course not. I could never be." She moved away from the door. She didn't want to confront Miles if he came out.

"Lydia?" Diana's voice sounded worried.

Lydia hurriedly wiped at the tears on her cheeks, but if Diana came any closer, there would be no concealing that she was crying. And come closer she did. Lydia kept her focus on Thomas, feigning the need to rearrange his clothing. He was starting to cry again—not a hungry cry or a tired cry but an upset one. Almost hurt.

But Diana wasn't fooled. She took one look at Lydia, put an arm around her, and guided her toward her bedchamber. "Come, my love."

Lydia didn't have the willpower to resist, and soon she was in Diana's room, being helped to the bed, where she sat with Thomas on her lap, both of them crying. Diana reached for the tasseled pillow that sat atop the coverlet and handed it to the baby. His crying stopped, and Diana wrapped her arm about Lydia, her hand stroking Lydia's arm.

"Trouble with Miles?" she asked softly.

Lydia looked at her. "How did you know?"

"Oh, Lydia," she said with a pained expression. "I know you. And I've been around the two of you enough to know that something has been amiss."

Lydia let out a sigh and shut her eyes. "Was it so obvious?"

Diana grimaced. "Is this little fellow the cause of your quarrel?" She nudged Thomas's cheek. He was playing with one of the tassels, attempting to bring it to his mouth, but instead it tickled his nose. His bewildered reaction brought a sad smile to Lydia's lips. But it soon faded.

"Tell me all about it," Diana said. "If you'd like to talk."

Since being married, Lydia had never confided her troubles to anyone but Miles. Her own mother had never had any trouble conceiving, and Lydia had heard her attribute the type of misfortune she and Miles were experiencing to the disfavor of God once or twice—enough to make Lydia reluctant to share their troubles with her.

Over time, Lydia had stopped confiding her struggles to Miles, too. How could she, when their situation was the root cause of her struggles? If she told him all her insecurities, he would have been too kind to tell her the truth of his own thoughts and feelings. He wouldn't have confirmed her suspicions even if they were true.

But the result was that Lydia had had no one to talk through things with—she had been a prisoner of her own mind and heart—and the burdens had been piling higher and heavier on her shoulders.

Whether it was right or not to confide in Diana, Lydia didn't know. But she couldn't keep things in any longer.

Besides, she could hardly have made things any worse than they already were.

Diana was quiet as Lydia tried to explain the gist of things, only interrupting to ask clarifying questions now and then and, once, finding a handkerchief for her. Thomas played contentedly with his pillow, for the most part, but by the time Lydia had finished, Diana was holding him in her arms, and he was fast falling asleep.

"Oh, Lydia," she said. "I am so terribly sorry."

Lydia swallowed down the lump in her throat and shook her head, guilt clawing itself above her frustration and hurt as she looked at the baby, peacefully sleeping now. "We made Thomas cry. We scared him with our arguing." She sniffed and put the handkerchief to her nose. "Miles wants to give Thomas to another family."

Diana looked down at the baby, biting her lip. "I *have* wondered sometimes if Miles is not perhaps a bit jealous of Thomas." She looked up at Lydia, who stared at her, her mind working through Diana's words.

"I don't mean this as a criticism of you, of course," Diana continued, "for I know you well enough to understand that you would never hurt anyone intentionally, but so much of your focus and your energy has been directed toward Thomas over the past two weeks. If things have been as you say between you and Miles, I imagine it might be painful for him to see you devoting yourself so fully to someone you only *just* came to know." She lifted her shoulders. "It would be a strange man indeed who would not have begun to doubt your feelings toward him after all you have been through. Just as you have doubted his."

Lydia fiddled with her fingers in her lap. She *hadn't* meant to make Miles feel neglected by her care for Thomas. At first, she had wished only to save Thomas from the situation they had found him in. It had been so wonderful, though, to hold a much-desired babe in her arms, to feel what she had longed for so long to experience.

But, even more than that, Thomas had soothed her loneliness. He had filled some of the hole left by what her marriage had become.

"I don't know how to fix things, Di," she said. "I don't even know if they *can* be fixed."

"Well," she said, rocking Thomas gently as he stirred, "I think you need to reassure him. Miles, I mean. He needs to know that you want above anything else to be with him, no matter what the future holds. Is that reassurance not what you wish for, as well? What you have been doubting? Of course, both of you want a child and an heir. But would you take an heir and a broken marriage with Miles over a happy marriage with him and no heir?"

Lydia shook her head. "No."

Diana sent her a sympathetic smile. "Then, you must decide how to ensure he knows your loyalty lies with him."

"But what if his does not lie with me? What if what he wants more than anything is an heir? And I can't give that to him?"

Diana gave a long sigh. "I do not think that is the case, Lydia. He loves you. I am sure of it. But he has been raised to think an heir his duty—a measure of his success. It takes time to change how you think of yourself. But I imagine he could bear with the prospect of the title passing to someone else if he was certain of *your* affection. It must be difficult indeed to feel as though he has lost both an heir and a wife."

Lydia put a hand to her mouth to stop its trembling. Diana was painfully right. In all Lydia's efforts to protect her own heart from rejection, she had rejected Miles. They were both mourning alone when they had promised to stand by each other.

Through Lydia's blurry vision, she looked at Thomas.

Had he become a thorn in the flesh for Miles? A painful reminder that his wife's affections lay elsewhere?

She adored Thomas, certainly. But more than she valued her marriage? Perhaps she was trying to do things backwards. She had been assuming that producing an heir was the only thing that could fix their marriage, but they could not bring a child into the home when their marriage was in shambles. Only look at the effect their fighting had had on Thomas.

"One more thing," Diana said, "and then I shall be silent. I promise. I remember well how it was to be with the two of you while you were courting and when you were first married." She smiled saucily. "It was almost nauseating how the love emanated from both of you. I particularly remember the night before your wedding, talking to you of the future—I can still recall how your eyes shone when you spoke of it." She tucked a strand of Lydia's hair behind her ear. "It is easier to dream up such a future than to create it, isn't it?"

Lydia nodded with her heart in her throat. The present was nothing like she had dreamed—or assumed—her future with Miles would be.

"Your life with Miles may not be what either of you anticipated, but that does not mean that there isn't joy and happiness to be found in it. It is simply a matter of working toward it—of looking for the opportunities that become available as other ones slip from your grasp. But first you must both decide that you *wish* for such a future. Together."

Lydia knew Diana was right. She only feared that perhaps Miles no longer wished for her to *be* part of his future. Perhaps too much damage had been done.

She needed to show him beyond any doubt that she would stay by his side if he would let her—that there was no reason at all to doubt her love or loyalty to him.

And she was beginning to understand what that might entail.

CHAPTER 21

Miles spent the morning in his bedchamber, lying on his back, staring up at the bed hangings above.

He had reacted with more anger than he had ever betrayed in his life. And he knew why. Hurt had been building within him for months now—longer, even. And seeing the pennyroyal, reading the letter from the solicitor...it had felt like all his worst fears being confirmed. No, not his worst fears. They were fears he had never even considered, for he had thought he knew Lydia too well to even contemplate such things. But seeing them had made him wonder how well he really *did* know her anymore.

Perhaps if he'd only had time to reflect before approaching her about his discoveries, he might have realized there were alternative explanations to the ones his mind and heart had jumped to.

But she had come in right then, just as he'd been in the middle of trying to understand it all. And he had done exactly what she'd said: made assumptions.

She told him she hadn't had her courses for months now. He knew how carefully she had always paid attention to such things—

indeed, he had as well. But it had been a long time since Miles had known the merest detail of what was happening in Lydia's body—or mind or heart, for that matter. And she had been carrying this burden alone.

He didn't know what to believe anymore. What did Lydia want? He could ask her, of course, but it had been so long since they had been fully truthful with one another in their communications, he didn't know if she would tell him her full and honest feelings. She might not feel safe doing so, particularly after all the awful things he had said to her just now. Even if she *had* been inquiring with the solicitor about divorce on his behalf rather than hers, he wouldn't blame her if she wanted the information for herself now. He had been a brute. He had accused her of infidelity, of all things. And with not a shred of justification.

He had let his own hurt drive him to hurt *her*, and that was so far from what he wanted. How would he make amends for it? He didn't know, but he had to try.

He swung his legs over the side of the bed and strode to the door between his and Lydia's rooms, rapping on the door. There was no response.

"Lydia?"

Still nothing. No sign of any movement.

With a nervous swallow, he opened the door, just enough to glance into the room. It was empty.

He shut it and hurried from his room. Where might she have gone? Perhaps she was with Diana and Mary. They hadn't been the best hosts to her sisters over the past few days. That was certain.

But she wasn't downstairs, either. Nor were Mary and Diana. Had they gone out, then?

Miles stopped one of the footmen in the hallway. "Have you seen Lady Lynham? Or her sisters?"

"They went out, my lord. Not fifteen minutes since."

"Thank you."

The footman bowed and continued about his duties, and Miles's shoulders dropped with the sigh he let out—a sigh of defeat. It was a trial to be patient when he wanted so badly to express what was inside him.

But he had no other option than to wait.

CHAPTER 22

Lydia cried softly the entire walk to her mother-in-law's with Thomas in her arms, bundled in two blankets. Diana and Mary walked beside her, both silent, both holding a small bag of the various belongings Thomas had acquired during his time with Lydia and Miles.

Lydia was grateful for their silence. Words could do nothing. Only time would heal this wound.

She should have prepared herself for it, protected her heart more by letting Jane care more for Thomas. She should not have allowed herself to become so attached. They had never intended to keep Thomas for more than a couple of weeks, and yet Lydia hadn't been able to stop herself from hoping for just that. She had come to realize she didn't need a child of her own flesh and blood; she just wanted a child to love.

But mostly, she wanted Miles. She could bear anything if she was confident of his love and his desire for a future with her.

The dowager baroness welcomed the sisters and Thomas with warmth and surprise, ringing for tea to be brought directly. Her eyes lingered on Thomas quite a bit, a fact which brought on an extra degree of hesitation from Lydia.

"We cannot stay long, I'm afraid," Lydia said as they sat down.

"Oh," said the dowager baroness as she prepared the tea. It was clear she was very curious about the reason for their unexpected visit.

But Lydia wasn't quite ready to tell her. She wanted to hold Thomas a little longer. Instead, she asked her mother-in-law questions about Miles's siblings, trying to keep her mind from the looming goodbye she would have to say to the warm, happy baby she held on her lap. Lydia had little heart for conversation, though, so she was grateful she had brought Diana and Mary with her, as they supplied it in ample measure.

But it couldn't be put off forever, particularly when Lydia had assured the dowager they wouldn't be staying long.

"He is looking much better than he did when we first came upon him, isn't he?" The dowager indicated Thomas with her head, smiling at him.

Lydia could only manage a nod.

Diana shot her an evaluative expression, as if trying to gauge whether Lydia intended to broach the subject they had come to discuss yet.

It was time.

"In fact, it is Thomas who brings us here," Lydia said, forcing herself to keep her composure. This was important. "Miles mentioned you had sent him a note about the situation you had found for him."

The dowager nodded, eyes watchful and curious.

"You have been kind to search such a thing out," Lydia said, even if *kind* wasn't the word she might have chosen. "I certainly don't wish to trouble you any further, but I was wondering if you might be willing to arrange for him to be conveyed there as well."

The dowager's brows rose. "Oh, I see. Yes, of course. I should be more than happy to do so."

Lydia swallowed and tried for a smile. "It is good of you. It may seem strange to you that I should wish for you to do it, but...I think I will find it easier the less I know."

Diana took her hand and held it between hers.

"As long as I know he will be well cared for," she said with a lump in her throat, "I shall be content." At least she hoped she would be, in time. This was necessary. She had to continue reminding herself of that fact. For the sake of her marriage, this was what was best. And for Thomas, as well. She would never forget the look of fright in his eyes when he had witnessed her argument with Miles.

"I understand," said the dowager baroness. She leaned forward and set a hand on Lydia's knee. "You are making the right decision, my dear. I hope you know that."

Lydia nodded, feeling her emotions fraying quickly.

Her mother-in-law looked at her with sympathy in her eyes and sat back in her chair. "I can have him conveyed there today if you wish it."

Lydia did not wish it, but there was no reason to delay things. It would only get more difficult the longer she waited, the more time she spent with him. He grabbed at her finger, shaking it up and down.

"I do wish it. May I just have a moment with him, though?" She asked it without looking up at the others.

"Of course," said the dowager, and she and Lydia's sisters rose from their seats.

Diana and Mary came over to Thomas first, taking turns kissing him on the top of the head.

"Goodbye, little ragamuffin," Diana said.

"Goodbye, sweet Thomas," said Mary.

They walked to the door, Diana with a sympathetic glance over her shoulder at Lydia.

"I'll only be a moment," Lydia said, trying for a smile. She would only *allow* herself that long.

The door closed softly, and she looked at Thomas, who was reaching for something nearby.

"Just you and I, my love," she said softly. "Just as it so often has been."

He flailed his arms, eyes on the buttons of her glove, and she let him play with it. He hadn't any idea what was happening. He was smiling, alert, and energetic. Everything that Lydia was not.

It was bittersweet, for it couldn't help but drive home the fact that Thomas wouldn't remember her. He would quickly adapt to whatever his new situation was, anxious to experience the new sights and sounds available to him there. He was adaptable; he was naturally good-tempered. Both those things would stand him in good stead.

As for her, though...she would never forget him.

CHAPTER 23

❄

The afternoon light was fading by the time Miles thought he heard the front door of the townhouse open. Standing before the mirror in his bedroom, he cocked an ear. It was an abnormally quiet entrance if it was indeed Lydia and her sisters. Diana's voice usually carried very well. Perhaps it wasn't them after all.

He had known a moment of panic earlier, wondering if it was possible that the three of them had left—left London—to travel to their home. His words to Lydia had been unforgivable. Perhaps he had driven her away and she had taken Thomas with her. He could hardly have blamed her if that was the case.

But a quick glance in Lydia's bedroom then Diana and Mary's told him that he was being ridiculous. They had clearly gone out for a simple walk or something of the sort. No doubt, they would be home in time for dinner, preferably far enough in advance that he could steal Lydia away to talk to her. To apologize.

It was why he was dressed for dinner so far in advance of the normal time. He wanted to be sure he was ready.

He heard footsteps in the corridor outside his room and muted voices. He hurried over to the door, opening it and stepping out into the corridor just in time to see Lydia slip into her bedroom. Diana and Mary stood in front of her door, faces somber as they glanced at Miles.

Lydia must have told them of his unkindness.

"I thought I heard you return," he said with a lump in his throat. He deserved that everyone should know what an awful brute he was.

"Yes," Diana said. Never had he seen her look so serious.

"Just in time to dress for dinner." He stepped toward Lydia's bedchamber. "Perhaps I can take Thomas so that Lydia can dress in peace."

Both Diana and Mary put a hand out to stop him.

"He isn't in there," Mary said.

Miles checked, letting his hand drop in the act of reaching for the doorknob. "She gave him to Jane, then?"

Diana shook her head, looking at him with something near to pity in her eyes. "He is gone, Miles."

He stared at her, stifling a nervous laugh. She clearly wasn't teasing. "What?"

"It is where we went," she said. "To your mother's. She is to take him to"—she lifted her shoulders—"wherever he is going."

Miles could only stare.

"I think Lydia needs a bit of time alone," Diana continued. "She said she will be down for dinner, though." She looked at Mary, and they gave Miles a little curtsy before making their way to their bedrooms.

Miles remained in the corridor for some time. Thomas was gone? Taken to his mother's? What did it mean? He wanted nothing more than to knock on her door and ask her himself. But Diana had said Lydia needed time.

Of course she did. If she had just said goodbye to Thomas....

He cringed, then his heart panged. *He* had never said goodbye. Had Lydia truly thought he wouldn't want to? Or that he wished her to give the baby up so quickly?

He hadn't meant to mention his mother's letter to her, but he had been so hurt by his discoveries in Lydia's room that he had done so. And at the worst moment. She had already doubted his affection for Thomas.

He strode back into his room, straining his ears to see if he could hear what he expected: soft cries from Lydia's room.

But he heard nothing. He sat on the edge of his bed, feeling as though he might go mad without any sign of what his wife was feeling or thinking, when finally, he heard footsteps in the corridor and what he imagined was Sarah's arrival to help Lydia dress for dinner.

He waited.

It was nearly twenty agonizing minutes later when the muffled shutting of the door followed by Sarah's withdrawing footsteps told him it was safe to go.

He knocked softly on Lydia's door. His heart was racing, but he couldn't help himself. It would be torture to go down to dinner with Lydia and her sisters, forced to make conversation about who knew what when all he wanted was to speak with Lydia alone.

When the door opened, he hungrily searched Lydia's face for signs of what she had been feeling. Her eyes were more red than usual, but she smiled at him when she saw him. It wasn't a normal smile. It was strange. Almost haunting.

"Lydia," he said. "I...your sisters said...." He found he couldn't get the words out. They stuck in his throat. Thomas was gone.

Her eyes flickered almost imperceptibly. "Come in," she said, opening the door wider.

He swallowed and stepped in, noticing the absence of the cradle beside the bed. The floor looked bare, the room too quiet. Just a few hours ago, it had been filled with Thomas's cradle and coos—and Miles's hurtful words.

"Lydia," he said, turning to her. "I am so unbelievably sorry. For all those things I said to you. I never meant for you to...I didn't mean any of it. I was just so terrified I had lost you."

She shook her head. "I should have told you, should never have kept anything from you."

"You kept it from me because you were afraid you couldn't talk to me. That is *my* fault."

"It is just as much mine. More, I think."

"But...but Thomas?"

She swallowed. "It is for the best. For him and for us."

He searched her face. "I don't understand."

"I need you to know, Miles," she said, and the first hint of emotion made her voice tremble. But she kept her chin up and her gaze on him. "I need you to know that I am here. With you. No matter what. I want a future with you, and I want to do whatever it takes to make it a happy one, even if it doesn't include children. I don't know if you still want me, but..." Her voice softened, and she averted her eyes. "I needed you to know that."

Heart in his throat and a burning in his eyes, he folded his wife in his arms, holding her tightly to him. "I have *always* wanted you," he said in a thick voice, muffled by her hair. "And I always shall."

They held each other—his face buried in her hair, hers in his shoulder—for Miles knew not how long. And with each passing minute, he felt some of the pain of the last few years falling away, until finally a knock sounded on the door.

"Lydia?" Diana's voice called. "Do you still wish to come down for dinner? Or shall I have it brought up to you?"

Miles and Lydia pulled apart, and Lydia brushed at her eyes, blinking quickly. "I am coming," she called out. "I shall meet you down there." She looked up at Miles, and he wiped at some of the remaining moisture on her cheeks then offered her his arm.

❄

They shared a bed that night, and though Lydia slept in his arms, sleep eluded Miles. His heart was uneasy. Lydia had smiled and talked throughout dinner and in the time they'd spent in the drawing room afterward, but she couldn't hide the hurt that lurked behind her smiles nor her glances at the door, as though Jane might bring Thomas to her anytime.

He felt it, too. Thomas's absence was deafening in the house. It seemed to change the entire atmosphere, and he couldn't be sure if it was just he and Lydia who felt it, or if Diana and Mary did too.

Twice that night, Lydia mumbled something in her sleep, arms cradling an imaginary baby. It was clear she had been keeping Thomas in her bed with her recently, and the sight of her hand searching for him drew Miles's brows together in a pained frown.

He pulled Lydia closer to him, which seemed to pacify her, for she settled into him, and her breathing calmed.

In the morning, he rose before her. His restless night had given him ample time to consider things, and he dressed in Lydia's room without the help of Bailey then made his way to his mother's.

She was sitting down to breakfast when he arrived, and from the surprised look on her face, he surmised that she had not been expecting him. There was no sign of Thomas. No doubt he was with one of the servants. Miles would ask to see him once he had spoken with his mother. He wanted a chance to say goodbye, if that was what he felt should happen by the end of his time with his mother.

"Miles," she said with a welcoming smile and gesture. "Come, sit, my dear. Have you breakfasted yet?"

He took a seat but made no move to reach for any of the food on the table. "No, but I am not hungry. Thank you."

She took her hand from the handle of the teapot with a sidelong glance at him.

"I won't be here long," he said. "I merely came to speak with you about Lydia's visit yesterday."

She took a sip from her teacup and raised her brows. "What about it?"

"What happened?" he asked.

She raised her shoulders up and blinked. "She came asking for me to take the child. But you knew that, of course."

"No, I didn't know."

"Didn't know? I assumed she had spoken to you about it."

He shook his head.

She reared back slightly, staring at him.

"We had an argument yesterday," he said, "and the next time I saw her was after her return. I had no idea..." He scrubbed a hand over his chin. "How did she seem?"

His mother tweaked her teacup slightly so that it sat at a more precise angle on the saucer. "She was very out of sorts. Which just goes to show that it was the right decision."

"I don't follow," he said.

"I only mean that she had become far too attached to the poor little thing. It was as if she thought he was *hers*." She sighed and gave a little shake of the head. "It will be much better this way."

Miles wasn't sure he agreed. "Where is he?"

"He is gone, of course. I took him myself yesterday just after the girls left. Just as I said I would."

Miles went still. "He is already gone?"

"Yes, my dear. I just said that. I didn't see the purpose to keeping him here any longer. The sooner he can habituate himself to his new situation, the better, surely."

Miles swallowed down his disappointment. "And what *is* that situation?"

She looked away from him, shifting in her seat. "Lydia specifically asked me not to tell her. I think you would be wise to follow her lead there."

"Mother," he said, feeling more uneasy than ever. "What *is* the situation?"

She didn't answer right away, and the result was that Miles's fists clenched and his heart raced. What had she done?

"I thought he would do best at the Foundling Hospital."

Miles was bereft of speech for nearly a minute. "The Foundling Hospital? But—but—they would not accept him."

She tipped her head to the side and pressed her lips together. "I do remember telling you that he surely would be if the right incentive was offered."

"Good heavens, Mother. Do you mean to say you bribed them to take him?"

Her brows snapped together. "What a vulgar way to phrase it. He is a foundling, Miles. Certainly there is no better place for him than the Foundling Hospital. Besides, they are always in need of more funds, of course. I was more than happy to contribute to the cause."

Miles covered his face with two hands, his stomach churning. What would Lydia say to know that *this* was the situation his mother had found? She would be horrified. It would devastate her.

"You are surely not angry with me," said his mother.

He stood, and the chair he was sitting in screeched dissonantly on the floor. "You made us believe you had found a family for him. You said *nothing* of the Foundling Hospital."

She rose from her seat. "The Foundling Hospital is a respectable institution. He will be well cared for, educated, trained to work. That is nothing for a child from heaven only knows where to sneer at."

Miles's jaw clenched tightly together, and he fought to keep the sharp words on his tongue from passing his lips. "You have done a great deal of damage, Mother. I have no desire to speak to you just now."

He turned on his heel and strode from the room, ill at the thought of revealing what he had discovered to Lydia.

CHAPTER 24

Lydia stayed in Miles's bed long past her usual time of rising. She was reluctant to enter her own room, and when she did, it was with slow steps and a heaviness in her heart. She didn't know where Miles had gone so early—she was only vaguely aware of him kissing her on the head, saying something in a reassuring voice, and rolling out of bed. The events of the day before had exhausted her, and she had quickly fallen back asleep.

But now she stood on the threshold of her own bedchamber, keenly aware of how empty her room felt. Where the cradle belonged, there was bare floorboard. It was the first thing she'd done when she had returned from the dowager's—had Jane take the cradle back downstairs.

It was silly for the empty space to affect her so. There had not *always* been a cradle there, after all. But it was the fact that there never would be again which wrung her heart and kept her feet from passing fully into the room.

She pulled her eyes from the vacant place and let them rove over the room. It felt different there. Not just because Thomas was gone. Something had shifted—perhaps not in the room itself. Perhaps it was within her. This place had felt like a refuge when she had first begun to occupy it. It was free of the conflict, the pain, and the failure she had begun to associate with the bed in Miles's room. In this bed, she had found rest and reprieve for a time.

Now, though, it was no refuge. It was full of loneliness. Even her time there with Thomas—so joyful while it had happened—was now awash in heartache and loss, as if someone had painted a glaze of sadness over the memories.

She *wanted* to leave it behind. She would gladly return to Miles's bed and share his room with him. It might not be entirely free of sorrow, but at least she wouldn't have to face it alone. That was the only comfort in all of this: Miles. When he had held her yesterday after her return from the dowager's, she had felt his love in a new way. It had given her hope that he would come to resign himself—or, heaven willing, may have already done so—to the likelihood that it would only ever be the two of them.

She took a determined step into the room, making her way toward the chest full of her clothing. This was something Sarah could have done, but Lydia wanted to do it herself. She wanted to experience it and let the significance of it wash over her.

A few at a time, she took her dresses and moved them to Miles's room, setting them on the bed. Then she pulled and hefted the chest there as well, setting it beside Miles's—where it used to be.

It took her nearly an hour to move everything to its new home—or old home, rather. Last of all, she went to the desk and opened the drawer. The letter from the solicitor sat inside, and the vial of pennyroyal rocked slightly beside it. She pulled out the letter and opened it, her eyes running over the words. It felt like a lifetime ago that she had opened it and read its contents. She had felt such disappointment then. It had been a crushing blow, the knowledge that she couldn't free Miles from his marriage to her.

What would things be like now if the solicitor's news had been different? If he had offered her hope rather than a door, locked and closed?

She took the paper to the fire and touched its edge to one of the flames, watching it consume the words little by little, then tossing it all onto the burning logs. The trail of fire turned the letter to ash and smoke, and with it, any thought Lydia had harbored of a life outside her marriage to Miles. If Miles would let them, they would envision a new future together.

The door to her room opened, and Miles appeared in the doorway. She smiled at him, but it flickered at the look on his face. He did not look happy.

"You're...in here," he said.

She nodded and rose, walking over to him. "Yes. But perhaps you noticed my trunk in *your* room. Our room," she said with a hint of shyness.

He glanced behind him, and the side of his mouth turned up at the corner. There was still sadness in it, though.

"I don't want to be in here anymore, Miles," she said. "I want to be with you."

He took her hands in his and looked down at her with what she could only describe as melancholy love. "I am very happy to hear that," he said.

"You do not look it," she said with a nervous lump in her throat.

He shook his head and looked down at their hands, rubbing his thumb along hers. "I have something to tell you. I was just at my mother's."

"Oh," she said, her mind immediately jumping to Thomas. "Is that where you went? I wasn't certain."

He nodded. "I wanted to see Thomas again and discover where she intended to take him."

Lydia swallowed, trying not to think of how much *she* wanted to see Thomas again too. "I am sorry, Miles. I should have allowed you to say goodbye before taking him. I was...I was afraid I would lose my nerve if I waited any longer. And I worried that you simply wanted him gone."

"Well, he *is* gone now. My mother took him yesterday."

Lydia nodded, taking in a large breath. It was just as the dowager had promised it would be. But the knowledge that Thomas was truly gone—completely out of reach—it still ached. She didn't want Miles to see just how much, though. She didn't want him to think she regretted it. She had done what was best for them.

"Lydia," Miles said, shutting his eyes with a brow furrowed in pain. "She took him to the Foundling Hospital."

Lydia's head snapped up, her eyes searching Miles's face.

"I am so sorry," he said. "If I'd had any idea it was what she intended, I would never have let her do such a thing. You must believe me."

She took a step back, blinking. "She couldn't have. They wouldn't accept him. They told us."

Miles lifted helpless shoulders. "She provided a donation they couldn't refuse. Whoever she spoke to must have made an exception."

She shook her head rapidly as images of the little boy she'd spoken to flashed into her mind—the one who hadn't said a word to her, who'd been wary of her. She shut her eyes to dispel the image, but it lingered there, and in the boy, she saw Thomas.

"We must get him," she said. "He can't stay there. He can't." She stepped back toward Miles and took his hands pleadingly in hers. "We must bring him back here and find him a family, Miles."

He nodded quickly. "Of course. I can go there now."

"Should I come?" she asked. She didn't know whether she wanted to or not. What if Thomas was already gone? What if they'd sent him to the countryside already and the errand was a futile one?

He searched her eyes. "I think you should remain here," he said.

He was right. She didn't know whether she would be able to keep her composure if she accompanied him. Miles had a more level head. He would be able to make them see reason. If it wasn't too late.

"I shall return as quickly as I can with news." He paused a moment then kissed her and left.

❄

"How shall I ever face her?" Lydia wrung her hands, pacing the floor in Diana's room as her sisters stood by.

"It was badly done of her, certainly," Diana said.

Lydia checked in place—perhaps the first time she had stopped moving since Miles left—and stared at her sister. "But...?" She knew the tone Diana was using.

Diana and Mary shared a look then Diana let out a gush of air. "I imagine it was done with good intention, Lydia. Just think, in the dowager's mind, the Foundling Hospital is precisely where Thomas belongs. She did not see what we saw when we went, and she has precious little attachment to the child. I imagine that Miles was foremost in her mind when she decided upon the course."

Lydia struggled to decide which part of this speech to respond to, but she settled on saying, "Miles?"

Mary nodded and stepped forward, almost as though they had rehearsed this conversation and the time had come for her part in the speech. "I am not saying that I agree with the course she took, for I don't, but I think it beneficial to at least *try* to see things from her perspective." She hesitated, her gaze shifting to the bed. "Come, sit, will you?"

Lydia complied, too curious how Mary or Diana might rationalize what her mother-in-law had done to resist.

Mary turned her body toward Lydia, looking at her intently. "You came to love Thomas quite dearly, didn't you?"

Lydia looked away, afraid if she responded to it, her anger might begin to give way to tears.

Mary nodded. "I know you did. It was apparent to all of us. He became like a son to you, I think. You want what is best for him, don't you?"

"Yes," Lydia managed to say. She had been unable to keep the doubts at bay since taking Thomas to the dowager's—doubts that, in acting in hers and Miles's interests, she was not acting in Thomas's, much as she might try to persuade herself. Would his new family truly be more loving than Lydia and Miles might have been? But there *was* no family. Her doubts had been merited.

"You know, then," Mary said, "what it is to be willing to do whatever it takes to ensure his happiness and success. That is precisely what Miles's mother was doing for him, I think. She has clearly been concerned about how Thomas would affect things here. It seemed she saw him as a distraction at best." She lifted her shoulders. "No doubt she believed she was doing what was best for Miles *and* you in taking Thomas to the Foundling Hospital."

The bell at the front door rang, and Lydia sighed. They hadn't had visitors in quite some time, but now that the weather was beginning to get a bit warmer, they could expect more.

A knock soon sounded on the door to Diana's room, and the three women shared curious glances. Diana went to open the door, revealing a footman was standing in the corridor.

His eyes searched the room, finding Lydia. "My lady, the dowager baroness has arrived and wishes to speak with you."

CHAPTER 25

❄

Lydia stared at the footman until his eyes began to shift uncomfortably.

"Very good," Diana chimed in, seeming to understand she could not count on Lydia to respond. "You may tell her we will be with her directly."

The footman bowed and left, and Diana shut the door, turning to Lydia.

"I cannot face her," Lydia said with a shake of the head. "I shall say something terrible; I just know it."

Diana shrugged. "Perhaps you should."

Lydia shot her an unamused look and continued to wring her hands.

"Well, not something awful," Diana continued, "but she should know that you are unhappy with what she did. Come, you may stay here a minute and gather your courage while Mary and I go see her."

Mary rubbed Lydia's back with a hand and rose. "You don't *have* to speak to her about it if you don't wish, you know."

"What? And just pretend nothing has happened?" Lydia shook her head. "Go ahead. I will be down shortly."

The door closed behind them, and Lydia sucked in a long, deep breath. What would she say to her mother-in-law? Had she really not thought that Lydia and Miles would discover what she had done with Thomas? Or had she known it would be too late by the time they had found out? What if Lydia had insisted upon knowing beforehand? Would the dowager have lied?

Perhaps Diana was right. Perhaps it was time for Lydia to have a more direct talk with her mother-in-law. She was turning over a new leaf with Miles, after all. It might be a good time for a bit of forthrightness.

Just the thought made her hands tremble. But she couldn't bear to continue as things were, with the dowager baroness inserting herself into their private matters, expecting an heir when it was clear there wouldn't be one. All this time, Lydia had been humiliated at what her mother-in-law would think of her when she finally realized Lydia couldn't give Miles an heir. She didn't want to live under that dread anymore. Better she know now and accustom herself to the fact.

Lydia rose from the bed, lifting her chin determinedly and making her way downstairs.

She checked at the door to the drawing room as the sound of the front door opening met her ears. She heard Miles's voice, and her heart raced. All thought of her mother-in-law fled, and Lydia hurried toward the entry hall just as Miles emerged from it into the corridor, Thomas in his arms.

Lydia's hand flew to her mouth, and Miles put out his free arm to welcome her into his embrace.

"When he saw me, he smiled so wide, I thought it would reach his ears," Miles said, and he handed off Thomas to her.

She pulled him into her arms and kissed his head. "I am so sorry, my love," she whispered. "So sorry."

He let out a loud squawk in reply and tugged on her hair, eliciting a laugh from both her and Miles.

"Did you have any trouble?" Lydia asked.

Miles shook his head. "Mr. Moss was understanding, and he was more than happy for me to take Thomas when I reassured him that the donation was theirs to keep."

A door opened down the corridor, and soon Diana, Mary, and the dowager baroness all appeared. Diana stopped, and Mary stumbled into her. All three of them stared with wide eyes for a moment, then Diana came rushing over.

"But...but..."

"Miles?" The dowager baroness's questioning voice broke through Diana's stuttering confusion. "What is this?"

"Or who is this?" Diana laughed as Thomas grasped her pointer finger and brought it to his mouth.

"Perhaps we could discuss this in the drawing room," Miles said.

His mother nodded with a hint of stiffness, and Diana and Mary launched into their excuses, pleading that they needed to begin packing their things for the journey home in two days.

Lydia felt her heart begin to patter against her chest, but Miles kept his arm around her and Thomas as they led the dowager baroness to the drawing room, and she knew a bit of comfort. Even if she couldn't rely upon Miles to put his mother in her place, she was glad to have him by her side while she did it.

Miles conveyed Lydia to the sofa and returned to shut the door behind his mother. Thomas reached for his favorite tasseled pillow, and Lydia obliged him by setting it on his lap. She wanted dearly to play with him, but there would be enough time for that after the encounter with her mother-in-law.

"I admit," said the dowager, "that I am at a loss to understand." She directed her gaze at Thomas, as though anyone was in any doubt of what she meant.

Miles came to sit beside Lydia. "I went to retrieve him. It is not the situation we wanted for him. I think you know that, Mother."

She inclined her head in acknowledgment. "I suspected as much, but—"

"But you saw fit to ignore our feelings on the matter," Lydia said, and she could feel her hands tremble as they held Thomas in place.

She didn't have to look at Miles to know that he would be showing signs of surprise. She had never countered her mother-in-law in anything.

The dowager blinked, eyes on Lydia. "I...I...I merely thought I was doing what was best. Surely you see that, to find a family who would take in the baby had its own risks. What if they found that they could not take care of him, after all? These are hard times, and I have known more than one instance where a well-meaning family overestimated their resources. If that happened, the baby would have been back on the streets. At least the Foundling Hospital would have avoided such a risk. These are difficult times, and the hospital would have given him the most certain opportunities."

"Then you should have discussed that with us," Miles said. "Instead, you concealed it."

"I had reason for doing so," she said. "It is difficult to see things clearly when one is so closely involved, as you both are. I have the advantage of a bit of distance." She looked at them with a sympathetic frown. "You cannot afford distraction."

"Distraction?" Lydia said.

The dowager baroness hesitated. "Well, yes. It seems to me that the two of you *have* been distracted by him. For you, my dear"—she nodded at Lydia—"I have wondered at times if you were not forgetting that he was not *yours*."

Lydia felt the blood pulsing through her veins, and when she spoke, it was with dangerous calm. "You believe Thomas is distracting me from what *truly* matters: producing an heir."

The dowager baroness said nothing, but the confirmation of Lydia's words was in her face—and her silence.

Hoping it might settle her temper, Lydia looked at Thomas, who was blissfully unaware of the discussion happening around him. She would not yell in front of him again. But she needed to make a few things clear.

"No doubt you mean well," Lydia said. It was true. The dowager *did* mean well in what she did. Diana's earlier words had not been lost upon Lydia. The dowager's primary interest was what she believed to be best for Miles, and she viewed Thomas as an impediment to that.

"But meaning well is not enough, my lady. You want Miles to find success in every arena of his life. I assume it is that desire which leads you to involve yourself in our affairs—to seek treatments that might help us to have children." She looked down at Thomas, who was chewing on a tassel, his hands covered in slobber. She swallowed and forced herself to sit up straight and meet her mother-in-law's gaze. "But the truth—unwelcome as it might be—is that there is unlikely to be an heir born to Miles and me."

Miles wrapped his arm about her and shifted closer, and the gesture reassured and strengthened her.

"I am nearly certain that I am unable to conceive," she said.

The dowager baroness stared at her, blinking slowly. "But…"

"I know it is difficult to hear," Lydia said. "Believe me, for it is even more difficult to *live*. But it is time that all of us faced up to the reality, I think."

Miles nodded. "I am at peace with it, Mother. And in time, you will be, too."

Lydia grasped at Miles's hand, her eyes flooding with tears. She had been craving those words for she knew not how long. Had he truly accepted it?

The dowager baroness sat forward on her seat, eyes flitting between them. "This resignation seems premature. Surely, there are other things that could be tried. Another doctor or—"

"No, Mother," Miles said flatly. "We do not wish to live our lives or burden our marriage with such things any longer. And we hope you will respect that—that you will leave these matters to us." He looked down at Lydia, and she nodded, holding his eyes, feeling her heart swell with love for him.

Miles's eyes roved over to Thomas. "That includes leaving Thomas's future in our hands. I believe I have already found another situation for him."

Lydia tensed, and her stomach dropped, but she tried to conceal it. What had she thought would happen? Miles had gone to retrieve Thomas so they could find him another home. She had merely thought she would have more time with him before having to say goodbye again.

Pushing down such thoughts, she looked at her mother-in-law. She thought she could see the hurt in her eyes, and, much as Lydia had longed to put the woman in her place for the last few years, the sight of her pain brought Lydia no joy.

She handed Thomas to Miles and went over to her mother-in-law, crouching in front of her. "I imagine you are feeling a number of things right now, my lady. I can understand many of those emotions myself, for I have sat with them these many years. They are very familiar to me. Whatever discouragement you feel at the knowledge that I cannot bear children, I have felt it ten-fold. Whatever regret you feel at Miles having chosen to marry me, I have anguished over both your regret and his ten-fold. But I want you to know that I intend to bring as much joy to Miles as I can manage. I may not be able to bear any children, but I will fight for him and his happiness, just as I know he will fight for me and mine. I want you to understand that I have his best interests at heart, just as you do. We have the same goal, and I hope you can find it in your heart to believe that, even if you cannot fully embrace me as a daughter-in-law."

The dowager shook her head and reached for Lydia's hand. "I do not regret that Miles married you, my dear. I admit it was not what I had wanted at the time." She smiled wryly. "Mothers always think they know better than anyone else, I think. But he chose you, and no one knows better than I how capable Miles is of making his own decisions. I am sorry if, in my determination to see him succeed, I have said or done things that led to unhappiness in you. That was never my intention. I know your happiness is integral to his. Please forgive me, my dear."

She stood and offered her hands to Lydia, pulling her up and into an embrace. In Lydia's ear, she whispered, "I would rather see Miles happy with a wife he loves and no heir than unhappy but with all the success in the world." She pulled away with a sigh and turned toward Miles.

Lydia hurried to take Thomas from him so that he and his mother could embrace properly.

"If you *do* find," she said as they walked her to the door, "that this situation you speak of will not serve, you need only say the word—"

"Mother," Miles said with a look that effectively shut her mouth.

She waved a hand as the footman opened the door. "Never mind that. You will manage quite well, I have no doubt."

"I rather think we will," Miles said, kissing Lydia on the head.

When the door had shut, they made their way out of the entry hall and toward the stairs, Thomas emitting loud squawks that filled the entire house, it seemed.

"They weren't gone for long," Miles said, "but I *did* miss those noises in his absence."

Lydia smiled, but she felt a bit of sadness. They would be gone again soon. She looked at Miles as they went up the stairs, his hand supporting the small of her back. "Miles, what situation *did* you find?"

They reached the top of the stairs, and he turned toward her, his brows furrowing. She could hardly stand to look at him, so nervous was she to hear his answer. She still wasn't certain she *wanted* to know.

"Well," he said, "that is something I wanted to discuss with you first. I am not sure you will like the idea."

She swallowed, waiting.

"I hoped," Miles said slowly, "that perhaps *we* might be his situation."

Lydia's eyelids flickered as she stared at him, and his mouth pulled into a tentative smile.

She blinked, heart thudding against her chest. "You are serious?"

He nodded. "I told you, my love. I missed his crowing and cooing."

She gave a shaky laugh then swallowed. "But, you are not doing this for me? I don't wish you to do it for me. I want to decide our future *together*."

He looked at her intently. "I *do* want this, my love. I am doing it for both of us."

Lydia looked at Thomas, who had availed himself of the corner of her dress and was sucking on it determinedly. "Do you hear that, Thomas? You are going to stay here. With us."

He gave no sign that he even heard her, and she looked back to her husband, unsure how to express what she was feeling. He seemed to understand and brought her into his arms.

It wasn't long, though, before he pulled away and looked censoriously at the baby. "You are very much in the way of things at the moment, little chap." He pulled him from Lydia's arms and set him on the floor, well away from the stairs. "We will be with you in a moment. I am sure I can count on your understanding." He stepped back to Lydia with a smile.

She looked at him through narrowed eyes. "You said you weren't sure I would like the idea. You delight in torturing me, don't you?"

He lifted a shoulder and donned an expression of faux-innocence. "Well, you *did* leave him with my mother to be taken to the Foundling Hospital without telling me. What else was I to surmise but that you wished to be rid of him?"

She smacked him playfully on the arm. "And you didn't tell your mother your plans."

He wrapped his arms around her waist and pursed his lips thoughtfully. "I thought we would save that revelation for tomorrow, once she's had a bit of time to process things. She's had quite a day, you know, between both of us being angry at her."

"I wasn't too unkind, was I?" Lydia asked nervously.

He shook his head. "Not at all. I nearly cheered when you said all of it. She will respect you the better for it having come directly from you."

She nodded, hoping he was right. "Are you absolutely certain, though, that you truly wish to have Thomas? I do love him, Miles, and I am exquisitely happy to think of him being ours, but"—she searched his eyes—"even more than that, more than anything, I want *you*. I want us to be together. You are my priority."

Miles took her face in both hands. "And you are mine. And that is what will make us good parents for Thomas."

Thomas suddenly yelled, and the sound echoed in the corridor. He stilled, eyes wide as the sound faded. He yelled again, and Miles and Lydia laughed.

He pressed his lips to hers, both of them smiling behind the kiss as Thomas emitted more of the same yells, increasing in volume.

"What a wonderful gift you have given me," Lydia said, her hands clasped behind Miles's neck.

"And a loud one," Miles said dryly with a sidelong glance at Thomas.

"I don't just mean Thomas," she said. "I *have* longed for a child. But having Thomas has made me realize that, even more, I was longing for *us*."

He closed his eyes, as though letting her words sink in, and his throat bobbed.

She rested her head against his chest, listening to the reassuring sound of his heartbeat. "I have missed you terribly, Miles," she said softly.

"And I you," he replied, pressing a kiss upon her hair. "I have wanted you from almost the moment I met you, Lydia. I have never stopped, and I never will. I promise you that. I will *always* love you, as long as I live."

"And I you," she said, and she rose up on her tiptoes. Miles met her lips eagerly, and they shared a kiss unlike one Lydia had ever experienced, meant to make up for every kiss they had missed.

A door opened down the corridor. "What is all the racket out here?" Diana checked when she saw Miles and Lydia lip-locked. "Oh."

They didn't pull apart right away, rather finishing the kiss slowly and gently. Reluctantly.

"A kiss like that may be worth an entire kissing bough of berries," Diana said with a mischievous smile. "It is just as well, for *I* have certainly not had any opportunity to take any berries, and it would be a shame for them to go to waste." She approached Thomas, crouching down and picking him up. "Have you been forgotten by these two lovebirds, my dear? How very cruel they are."

"He is staying, Di," Lydia said, holding Miles's hand tightly in hers and standing beside him.

"Of course he is," Diana said, rubbing her nose against Thomas's. "Where else would he go? He belongs here." With Thomas in her arms, she made her way back toward her room.

"Di!" Lydia called with a baffled smile. "What are you doing?"

"Taking him with me," she called over her shoulder. "I rather think you two have a few more berries-worth of kiss left in you."

Lydia looked up at Miles, who chuckled as the door to Diana's room closed with a *thunk,* cutting short Thomas's unintelligible talking.

"And *I*"—Lydia led Miles toward his bedchamber and opened the door—"rather think she is right."

EPILOGUE

DECEMBER 18, 1815

The carriage clattered and jostled over the cobblestones, finally rolling to a stop after passing through the wrought-iron gates.

Thomas slapped a hand against the coach window, and Lydia took in a deep breath.

"Are you ready?" Miles asked, peering over her shoulder at the prospect of the Foundling Hospital. There was no snow on the ground this year—December had been mild. They would make their way to Staffordshire tomorrow, where Lydia's own family would join them for Christmastide.

Lydia looked at Miles with a smile and nodded, though butterflies flapped within her stomach in mixed anticipation and nervousness. "I am."

He helped her down from the carriage then turned for Thomas, who was ready to attempt the descent himself. He was determined to demonstrate his skills as a walker—and an aspiring runner—whenever the opportunity presented itself.

"No, no, Tommy," Miles said, helping him down. "We will practice that another day. We mustn't keep them waiting."

Two wagons waited behind their coach, and servants emerged, ready to be instructed.

"Wait here," Miles instructed them. "We will be out shortly."

The three of them headed toward the main building just as a queue of children filed out of the edifice to their right. Lydia slowed her pace, and Miles followed suit. Together, they watched the children cross the courtyard to the building opposite, many of them sending curious glances toward the three of them.

Lydia sighed, and Miles looked at her with an understanding grimace, while Thomas watched the children, entranced into stillness for a brief moment.

"I wish we could help them all," Lydia said, looking at each face.

"I know, my love. And we *are*. Not as much as either of us might wish, perhaps, but still. They will have a happier Christmas for our gifts."

He was right, of course. The gesture might be small, but it would mean *something*. "I wish we could deliver them ourselves like we did last year," Lydia said as they continued to the doors, "but I suppose the important thing is that they receive the gifts."

Once inside, they were greeted by Mr. Moss, who smiled at them genially.

"Lord and Lady Lynham," he said. "We are honored to welcome you here again."

Miles inclined his head with respect as Thomas wriggled in his arms. Miles set him down, and a large grin spread across the toddler's face at the freedom presented. Lydia couldn't help but think how grateful she was that this would be his experience of the hospital—visiting with his mother and father. Just a month ago, the Court of Chancery had granted Miles legal guardianship over Thomas. Things might have been quite different for him.

"There are two wagons in the courtyard," Miles said to Mr. Moss.

"The servants are waiting to be instructed where to deposit the gifts they contain."

Mr. Moss instructed one of his men to go attend to it, and they were left alone with him again.

Thomas hung on Lydia's skirts, and she gave Miles a light nudge with her elbow.

He cleared his throat. "As for the other matter, I trust all is in order."

Mr. Moss nodded. "Indeed. I will warn you that he can be a bit difficult. He has never been one for many words and will need time to accustom himself—a significant amount of time, perhaps."

Lydia nodded hurriedly. "Of course. We quite understand."

Mr. Moss hesitated a moment then turned, disappearing through a door behind him.

Lydia grabbed Miles's hand and squeezed it, and he returned the pressure.

The door opened again, and Lydia straightened. Mr. Moss emerged and, behind him, a boy. He was much taller than Lydia had remembered. He was ten years old now, as far as the hospital had been able to estimate. His dark hair looked to have been recently cut, so blunt were the ends, sitting across his forehead. He put a hand to the hair, pressing it down in a self-conscious gesture that wrung Lydia's heart. She knew what she would see on that hand—scars from lashings, hopefully faded by now.

"Good day, Matthew," Lydia said, and her voice trembled, part emotion, part nerves.

He said nothing, holding his hands behind his back and looking down.

"Come, Matthew," Mr. Moss said. "Lady Lynham is speaking to you. It is uncivil not to respond."

"Good day, ma'am," said the boy in a reluctant, dark tone, while his eyes looked anywhere but her face.

She and Miles shared a look. This would be difficult. They had known that. But, when they had decided to take in another child,

Lydia had immediately known that it was Matthew she wished to welcome into their home.

"Thank you, Matthew. There is no need to speak if you don't wish to, though. I understand this must all be very strange to you."

He said nothing, and, with a tight-lipped grimace, Mr. Moss took Miles with him to sign a few papers, leaving Lydia, Thomas, and Matthew alone.

Thomas toddled over to Matthew, who watched him with wariness. He had likely never been around a baby before. There would be many new things for him to get used to.

Thomas tugged on Matthew's finger, and Lydia came over, pulling Thomas away. "He likes you. He wants to play with you, I think. It is one of his favorite games, see?" She put out her palm, and Thomas smacked it with his own hand.

The corner of Matthew's mouth pulled up, but he quickly controlled it.

The momentary flicker gave Lydia hope, though. Perhaps Thomas would do for Matthew what he had done for Miles and Lydia—generating interaction and joy where it had long been absent.

Miles emerged shortly and came to Matthew's side. "Are you ready, Matthew? Our carriage is just outside, waiting for us."

Matthew's eyes showed the first signs of fear, and he looked to Mr. Moss, who nodded.

"They will take good care of you, Matthew," said Mr. Moss.

Matthew gave a slight nod, and they bid farewell to Mr. Moss.

They let Matthew climb into the carriage first, and he scooted as far into the corner as he possibly could. Miles took the seat beside him, giving him his space. Lydia wished she could wrap her arms around the boy and reassure him that all would be well.

All in good time.

"We are very happy to have you joining our family, Matthew," Miles said as he knocked his hand to signal the coach driver.

"We truly are." Lydia pulled Thomas back down onto the seat as he tried to stand up. "I hope that you will be happy with us, too. In time."

Matthew remained silent, and Miles smiled at Lydia across the coach. This would be a new adventure together, and she was grateful she would have Miles beside her for it.

THE END

ALSO IN THIS SERIES

Belles of Christmas: Frost Fair
- Her Silent Knight by Ashtyn Newbold
- All is Mary and Bright by Kasey Stockton
- Thawing the Viscount's Heart by Mindy Burbidge Strunk
- On the Second Day of Christmas by Deborah M. Hathaway
- The Christmas Foundling by Martha Keyes

Belles of Christmas: Masquerade
- Unmasking Lady Caroline by Mindy Burbidge Strunk
- Goodwill for the Gentleman by Martha Keyes
- The Earl's Mistletoe Match by Ashtyn Newbold
- Nine Ladies Dancing by Deborah M. Hathaway
- A Duke for Lady Eve by Kasey Stockton

AFTERWORD

Thank you so much for reading *The Christmas Foundling*. I hope you've already had the opportunity to read and enjoy the other books in the series.

I have done my best to be true to the time period and particulars of the day, so I apologize if I got anything wrong. I continue learning and researching while trying to craft stories that will be enjoyable to readers like you.

If you enjoyed the book, please leave a review and tell your friends. Authors like me rely on readers like you to spread the word about books you've enjoyed.

If you would like to stay in touch, please sign up for my newsletter. If you just want updates on new releases, you can follow me on BookBub or Amazon. You can also connect with me on Facebook and Instagram. I would love to hear from you!

OTHER TITLES BY MARTHA KEYES

If you enjoyed this book, make sure to check out my other books:

Tales from the Highlands

The Widow and the Highlander (Book One)

The Enemy and Miss Innes (Book Two)

The Innkeeper and the Fugitive (Book Three)

Families of Dorset

Wyndcross: A Regency Romance (Book One)

Isabel: A Regency Romance (Book Two)

Cecilia: A Regency Romance (Book Three)

Hazelhurst: A Regency Romance (Book Four)

Phoebe: A Regency Romance (Series Novelette)

Regency Shakespeare

A Foolish Heart (Book One)

My Wild Heart (Book Two)

True of Heart (Book Three)

Other Titles

Of Lands High and Low

The Highwayman's Letter (Sons of Somerset Book 5)

A Seaside Summer (Timeless Regency Romance Book 17)

The Christmas Foundling (Belles of Christmas: Frost Fair Book Five)

Goodwill for the Gentleman (Belles of Christmas Book Two)

The Road through Rushbury (Seasons of Change Book One)

Eleanor: A Regency Romance

Join my Newsletter to keep in touch and learn more about British history! I try to keep it fun and interesting.

OR follow me on BookBub to see my recommendations and get alerts about my new releases.

ACKNOWLEDGMENTS

I have my own life experience to thank for this work, first and foremost. It has shaped me in ways I perhaps never wanted but certainly needed. I acknowledge God's hand in that and in turning pain into joy as only He can.

My husband has lived through it all with me, and he continues to support me in the most winning ways as I've gotten this story down.

Thank you to Micah, Jonah, and Zachariah for teaching me so many of the lessons in this book. You are everything to me.

Special thanks to my fellow authors in the series: Ashtyn, Kasey, Mindy, and Deborah. You are the dream team to work with. Thank you to my critique group partners for helping me iron out kinks and issues in the early stages.

Thank you to my editor, Jenny Proctor, for her wonderful feedback—I'm so glad I have you!

Thank you to my beta readers and Review Team for your help and support in an often nerve-wracking business.

And as always, thank you to all my fellow Regency authors and to the wonderful communities of The Writing Gals and LDS Beta Readers. I would be lost without all of your help and trailblazing!

ABOUT THE AUTHOR

Martha Keyes was born, raised, and educated in Utah—a home she loves dearly but also dearly loves to escape whenever she can travel the world. She received a BA in French Studies and a Master of Public Health, both from Brigham Young University.

Word crafting has always fascinated and motivated her, but it wasn't until a few years ago that she considered writing her own stories. When she isn't writing, she is honing her photography skills, looking for travel deals, and spending time with her husband and children. She lives with her husband and twin boys in Vineyard, Utah.

Made in United States
Orlando, FL
24 November 2021